A CHRISTMAS TO REMEMBER

EVERGREEN HOLLOW CHRISTMAS BOOK THREE

FIONA BAKER

JOIN MY NEWSLETTER

If you love beachy, feel-good women's fiction, sign up to receive my newsletter, where you'll get free books, exclusive bonus content, and info on my new releases and sales!

CHAPTER ONE

Margo Stoker couldn't remember there ever having been a morning when she wasn't excited to get to work.

She knew she was lucky in that regard. She'd spent her whole life so far, ever since college, doing exactly the job that she'd hoped to do. She'd finished a double major in journalism and photography, landed a killer internship in New York, and then gotten an excellent job at a magazine just outside the city, in New Jersey. She had an apartment she loved, a fulfilling job, and woke up every day excited to find out what it would hold.

There were things that bothered her, of course. Things she tried not to think too hard about, because she knew she was fortunate in so many respects. She'd always been good at that—at staying positive.

Which was why, today, she felt justified in letting herself fall apart just a little.

The day had started out fine. She'd gotten up at seven a.m., the way she always did, throwing on leggings and a long sweater with a graphic of an old Polaroid camera on the front, getting in a series of quick morning stretches while her coffee brewed. She'd drunk it with a heavy helping of creamer standing over the counter while shoveling bites of a bagel and cream cheese into her mouth between sips, swapped out the leggings for jeans and her Docs, grabbed her leather messenger bag, and hurried out to where her trusty Subaru was parked.

She'd been driving the same car for ten years, and it had yet to fail her. All-wheel-drive in New Jersey came in handy, especially this time of year, and if she needed to take photos anywhere within driving distance, the car could take her anywhere she needed to go. It often had. She liked to mix things up in her life—her outfits, her hairstyles, her grocery options for the week—always feeling a little restless and in need of trying new things, but her car and her camera were her two standbys. Neither had needed replacing in years, and she knew she could rely on them.

Change was good, and variety even better in her opinion, but a girl needed to have a couple of things she could count on.

As she drove, merging onto the highway and turning the radio to a Christmas jazz channel, she mulled over her work for the day. She'd been excited all weekend to get into the office, even spending a few hours going over some notes at home while she caught up on TV shows. She had a great scoop on some fossils that had recently been discovered in the Caribbean, and she was itching to show what she'd found to Richard, her boss. She was pretty sure no one else had covered it yet, and she wanted this assignment. She'd only just gotten back from Egypt a week ago, but she thought she wouldn't mind spending the cold winter months somewhere tropical one bit. She'd grown up in a cold climate, and she'd made it a personal goal to spend as many winters somewhere warm as she could manage.

Richard was always pleased with her work, and he usually gave her the assignments she wanted. She felt confident that this wouldn't be any different.

She pulled into the parking lot of the magazine's building, fishing her building pass out of the center console and grabbing her bag. The parking lot was thick with snow, not all of it completely plowed yet, and she shivered as she stepped out into the cold. She already missed the dry heat and sand of Egypt, and she was eagerly anticipating the possibility of crystal white sands, humidity, and tropical drinks at the end of every day.

A lot of the time, her job didn't really feel like work at all.

She hurried into the building, dropping her bag at her desk and shrugging off her coat and gloves. She hadn't even had a chance to sit down when she saw Richard walking toward her, and she beamed at him, hurrying to meet him.

"Morning!" she said brightly. "I have something I want to show you if you have a minute."

"Actually, I wanted to talk to you as soon as you got back, Margo. If you'll come into my office for a minute?" He gestured toward the glassed-in room, and Margo frowned. He sounded oddly serious, but this time of year could be stressful for everyone. Or maybe he had an assignment for her already, and it was one he knew she wouldn't like. A piece that required her to go somewhere even colder, like Russia. Or Antarctica.

She shivered, hoping she was wrong as she followed him into the office.

"Sit down, please." Richard smiled, but she thought it looked tight around the edges, a little forced. "How was Egypt?"

"Hot. Much better than here." Margo sank down into a chair, looking at him curiously. "What's going on?"

He let out a slow breath, sitting down in his own leather chair behind his desk. "I have some bad news, Margo. It's the worst time of year to have to tell you this, I know, but I really have no other options. We're downsizing the company, and having to make significant cuts to staff. And unfortunately, you're one of the staff members that we're going to have to let go."

She wasn't sure she'd heard him right. It was the buzzing in her ears, maybe, that made her think he'd said something else. He couldn't possibly have said she was being *fired*.

"What? Surely you don't mean..."

"I'm sorry, Margo." He did sound genuinely sorry. But she still couldn't believe it.

She'd heard through the grapevine that the company was struggling. There had been a few internal emails among the other staff that she'd seen while she was in Egypt, recently, that she probably wasn't supposed to have been cc'd on but hadn't been able to keep herself from reading.

But she was sure it was just an overreaction, that someone had heard about the difficulties and were blowing it out of proportion. She'd been sure that the company would pull through, and it would all be fine.

But it seemed like she'd been too wrapped up in her work to realize how bad things had really gotten.

"So that's it?" She bit her lip, feeling the sudden urge to cry. She hadn't cried in ages, but she could feel the heat behind her eyelids, threatening.

Her pitch for the article about the fossils was crumbling before her eyes. Her sunny winter spent in the tropics doing her job, the thing she loved best, was vanishing. Her *everything* was falling apart. Her whole life was her job because she genuinely loved it. If she'd ever been married to anything, it was her work as a journalist. She'd thrown her all into it, for fifteen years of her life.

And now it was over. Just like that. She was being shown the door—politely, but still the door, nonetheless.

"I'm really sorry." Richard stood, and she could see that there wasn't going to be any drawn-out conversation over it. "You'll get a severance package, as will everyone affected by the layoffs. It'll be as generous as we can manage, given the circumstances. I know being laid off during the holidays is terrible. Believe me, if there was any other way..."

"I know." Her voice sounded hollow to her own ears, as though she was speaking down a hallway. "I understand."

She didn't, not really. But she wanted to be out of that office, which suddenly felt small and cramped, like it was closing in around her. She wanted to be alone, so she could think. But first, she had to wrap up any loose ends that needed to be done before she packed up her things for the last time.

This might be her last day at the magazine, but what she would leave behind would be the result of her whole life's work so far. She didn't want to finish off her last assignment sloppily just because she knew she wouldn't be coming back.

It took her all day to finish those last items on her to-do list. She'd planned, this morning, on having them done in an hour or two, on polishing the last lines of the Egypt article and sending the final draft over to Richard, and then waiting on pins and needles to hear his reaction to her pitch about the fossils. But instead, the work that should have taken her no time at all crawled by, because she couldn't focus. She couldn't concentrate.

There was no plan B for her. No backup. Why would she have ever needed one, when she'd never planned on doing anything else?

She hadn't planned on looking for work at another magazine. There had been no reason to. Richard was always happy with her articles, she always loved her assignments, and she'd always felt fulfilled. She hadn't thought about what she would do in a situation like this because... well, she'd just never thought about it. She'd been happy, and she'd never been the type to plan for a rainy day when it always felt like the sun was shining.

Now, she guessed she was paying for that. She could just imagine what her older sister Caroline would have to say about her lack of foresight. Nothing positive, that was for sure.

She had no idea what she was going to do.

When the last of her things were packed up, she said goodbye to her colleagues, promising to keep in touch even though she knew that no one probably would. They were all bad at seeing each other outside of the office, no matter how many lunches or happy hours they tried to coordinate.

Everyone who worked at the magazine was always in different places at different times, flung across the globe, in too many different time zones to even organize a video call for a digital happy hour. She didn't think that inability to schedule a time that worked for everyone was going to change just because some of them were unemployed now.

She handed in her building pass to Richard, nodding as he explained that he would send her severance check in the next couple of days, and asked if she wanted it to go to her home address. She didn't have any idea where else he would send it, so she kept nodding.

It hit her, as she did, that she was going to be home for the foreseeable future. For Christmas. *Home for the holidays* didn't sound all that good when her apartment was more like a hotel room than a home.

That hit her all over again when she walked in her front door, tossing the keys down on the kitchen counter that was only a few steps from the foyer. She never bothered to really look at or think about her apartment, but she stood there for a few long seconds, looking at it with fresh eyes.

The plain, almost empty countertops except for a coffee maker, because she was rarely home long enough to bother with learning to cook, and she got takeout most of the time when she was. The furniture that she'd haphazardly bought from IKEA when she'd moved in because it was cheap and serviceable, and why did she care how it all looked when she rarely saw it?

There was nothing cozy about her home, she realized. No throw pillows on the couch or soft blankets to cuddle under when she watched TV. Her bookshelf had a smattering of books on it, ones that she'd bought to take along with her on flights, but that was all. No candles. Those cheap white blinds on the windows instead of curtains. And she knew what she would find once she went into the bathroom or bedroom. It would be more of the same.

Whatever shampoo and bodywash she'd grabbed off the shelf at the grocery store to keep at home, since most of the time she lived off whatever was available at hotels—or, in rougher places, travel-sized bottles that she threw into her luggage. A plain duvet and pillows she'd grabbed when she moved in, more IKEA furniture. The place was neat and clean, but there was nothing homey about it.

It definitely wasn't a place to crash.

She went to the fridge, pulled a Chinese restaurant flyer off it, and dialed the number. One order of sesame chicken and crab Rangoon later, she rummaged in her fridge for one of the beers she'd bought when she'd gotten back into town, trying to ignore the fact that the only things in there besides that were the cream cheese she'd gotten to go with her breakfast bagels, creamer, and some ketchup and mustard bottles bought ages ago, along with a bottle of flavored seltzer water.

I don't have a home, she thought glumly as she popped the cap off her beer and retreated to the couch to wait on her takeout.

It had never bothered her before. The whole world had been her home. She didn't need a plush apartment or matching throw pillows when tomorrow she could be in Spain, the week after that in London, and three months later in Morocco. Home was wherever she was sent, and she had always felt like it made her special, that she could be comfortable anywhere. She liked that about herself, that she could be happy living out of a suitcase, putting down roots for a little while and then pulling them up again to replant herself somewhere new.

Except apparently this was the one place she *couldn't* feel at home. Her own apartment.

Maybe not the only place.

The thought popped grimly into her head as the

knock came at the door to let her know that her dinner had been delivered. She went and collected it, bringing it back to her coffee table to eat, but she didn't have much of an appetite. Not even the scent of her favorite comfort food could entice her to eat after the day she'd had.

She flicked on the TV to the first channel that came on, wanting to distract herself. But the channel it had been set to was playing *It's A Wonderful Life,* and she immediately felt her spirits sink.

A rush of sadness and a hint of desperation washed over her as the black and white images flickered on her screen, as Jimmy Stewart talked about lassoing the moon. She could remember this movie being on in the background a dozen times while she and her sisters had made Christmas cookies when they were younger.

It was their mother and Caroline's favorite movie, even though Nora preferred *How the Grinch Stole Christmas,* and Margo had always liked *Rudolph the Red-Nosed Reindeer.* She hadn't watched the movie in years, but she could still have recited every line. It brought back a flood of memories instantly, from a time when she was completely unafraid and before her heart had been shattered into a million pieces.

In that moment, she found herself making a snap decision. She hadn't spoken to her sisters in months, and her mother in at least that long. But she decided as she watched George Bailey try to sweet talk Mary, that she was going to go back to Evergreen Hollow for a few days. Not through Christmas. She had no intention of staying that long. But she knew she didn't want to be where she was right that second. And it would give her time to decide where she wanted to spend the holiday.

A little time to regroup. That was all she needed.

And then she would be fine.

CHAPTER TWO

It was one in the afternoon, and Spencer Thorpe, Evergreen Hollow's resident doctor, was ready to take his lunch break.

The morning had been full of patients. A successful morning, with nothing more serious than a light case of the flu, but a busy one. The winter always seemed to be busy, between kids coming down with various bugs and winter injuries, and the usual cold-weather aches and pains that tended to plague Evergreen Hollow's older residents. But he was happy to help. He enjoyed his work, and had done ever since he'd taken over his father Alan's practice a year ago. He did, however, think there was something to the idea of hiring an extra nurse. Just so he got to actually take a lunch break more often.

As if to underline that thought, he heard the door open just as he was about to shrug out of his white coat. He stepped out into the waiting room instead, since the receptionist was still on lunch herself. It was just him, for now.

Sabrina Burns was walking toward him. She was hard to miss, with her bright red hair. He would have known her even if he hadn't been able to see her tight, harried expression.

"Oh, Spencer! I'm glad to see you." She dusted a little snow off her coat, talking rapidly. "I have a prescription to pick up? For the anti-anxiety medication."

"Ah. Hold on. It should be here in your file." He circled around the desk, thumbing through the yellow folders. "You know," he added wryly as he found hers and opened it up, "you probably wouldn't need it if you weren't so nosy, and didn't get so worked up about other people's business." He smiled as he said it, taking a little of the sting out of the words. "But, I'm a doctor, not a miracle worker. So there's no way for me to reverse one of your most prominent character traits, I'm afraid." He held out the prescription to her.

Sabrina sniffed, taking it out of his hand, but there was a small smile at the corners of her mouth.

"You're lucky you're so handsome," she teased. "I wouldn't let anyone else talk to me like that."

"I know." Spencer leaned on the side of the counter, raising an eyebrow. "But I'm your doctor. It's my job to dispense medical advice."

"Well, it's always good advice. You really have been such a great addition to the community over this past year." Sabrina flashed him a brilliant smile. "I really don't know what we did without you, before. The only thing I'm wondering is how you came to us without a Mrs. Thorpe in tow—or barring that, how you managed to spend a whole year here without one of the Evergreen Hollow ladies locking you down."

Spencer chuckled, side-eyeing her as he closed the file and tucked it away. "I just haven't found the right person," he said simply. "I'm sure if it's meant to be, it will happen."

"But in San Francisco?" Sabrina clucked her tongue. "I can't believe out of all those eager ladies that there must have been to choose from, you couldn't find *anyone*. A whole city! I'm sure your work kept you busy, but there must have been *someone*."

He shook his head, stepping back around the desk. "No one important enough to mention," he assured her. "Besides, there were more choices, you're right. In everything, really. But I love the quiet life here. I can hear myself think, and pause to appreciate the simple beauties in life. The girls I met there weren't interested in a slower-paced life. Whoever I choose to spend the rest of my life with would need to be."

"So you always intended on coming back here?" Sabrina pressed, and Spencer chuckled.

He knew she'd keep pressing as long as she thought she could get information about him. It was just her nature. She loved gossip, and she loved knowing as much as she possibly could about the residents of Evergreen Hollow.

She hadn't gotten nearly enough out of him over the past year, and anyway, a year of residence was practically a week compared to how long most people had lived here. He was still basically a newcomer, in Evergreen Hollow time.

"It was always in the back of my head," he said. "I thought I'd come back when the time was right. Which is a practice I apply to most things. Nothing should be rushed. When it's right, it'll happen."

He could tell that wasn't the answer Sabrina wanted from the way she wrinkled her nose. But he didn't have the kind of gossip he knew she was hungry for. And he wasn't overly interested in discussing his personal life, or the lack thereof.

"Well, I'll keep an eye out for prospects to send your way," Sabrina said, tucking the prescription into her purse. "And I'll be sure to wait for a thank you when you find the love of your life because of me."

Spencer laughed at that. "I'll say thank you now, for thinking of me. But I should probably get to lunch before someone else comes through that door."

"Oh! Of course. Sorry for keeping you." Sabrina pushed the door open, heading back out into the cold, and he followed her as he exchanged his white doctor's coat for a heavier black peacoat to ward against the frigid air outside.

Despite the chill, he opted to walk to Rockridge Grill for lunch. It was only a couple of blocks away, and the nurse would be back from her own break soon. He figured she could handle it long enough for him to get lunch, and the Tuesday special at Rockridge Grill was always a meatloaf sandwich. He'd been thinking about it all day, hoping he'd be able to duck out long enough to grab one.

It was yet another thing he liked about Evergreen Hollow, he thought. Back in San Francisco, taking a lunch break just wasn't a possibility. He was lucky to scarf down half a cafeteria sandwich that someone else brought him, or get a bag of chips between appointments. Taking even a half hour to go and get a hearty lunch was unheard of. He'd worked days, more often than not, where he got to the hospital before breakfast and left after dinner.

The work had been fulfilling in many ways. He'd worked on cases far more difficult than he ever saw here, and felt the glow of solving someone's problem, of giving them a new and better quality of life afterward. He'd used his skills to their fullest, and often been challenged. But he'd been doing that for years. And he'd started to burn out, as much as he'd known he wasn't supposed to admit it.

He'd been glad, deep down, for a reason to come home. A reason to slow down, to live and work somewhere where an emergency was the exception, not a multiple-times-per-day occurrence. Where he could breathe, and start to think about what else he might want for his life beyond just work.

A relationship might be part of that. He was in no hurry, and had no desire to rush it. But he'd definitely thought about what it might be like to have time to *really* date someone. He wouldn't have to let someone down any longer by canceling dates because he couldn't leave the hospital in time, or having to slip out of bed at three in the morning because he was on call, or abandon a date in the middle of dinner. He wouldn't come home exhausted, night after night, in no mood to go out to a movie or drinks or the theater because he'd lost a patient, or had to give someone bad news, or repeated that multiple times throughout the day.

If he found someone, he thought, he might be able to form a long-lasting relationship. To have a partner, get married, possibly even have children in the future. He didn't know if those things were in the cards for him, but they were at least possibilities now.

He had a feeling that it wasn't going to be Sabrina though, who paired him with the right woman.

More often than not, he thought instead, the right one would arrive when he least expected it.

CHAPTER THREE

Nora tucked her scarf a little closer around her neck, feeling the bite of the cold. She was headed to The Mistletoe Inn for a visit, and even though she knew her mother would say she should have taken the car, she'd wanted to walk. She'd gotten used to walking pretty much everywhere in town over the last two years, and at five months pregnant, she had been told by Evergreen Hollow's resident doctor that exercise was good for the baby. She had been using it as an excuse to visit the inn more often than not, lately.

Truthfully, there was more to it than that. She had enjoyed being back home with her family ever since she'd decided to stay in Evergreen Hollow, but there had been a particular comfort in being near them over the last few months. The prospect of being a mother was an exciting one, but it was also an unfamiliar, and a little bit scary, time. She was looking forward to it, but she was also nervous. Being with her mother always eased her nerves, and it helped that she and her older sister Caroline were closer now too. Especially since Caroline had met the local firefighter, Rhett Dawkins, and fallen in love last Christmas, her sister had softened up a great deal.

She always loved Evergreen Hollow no matter the time of year, but the holidays always felt particularly special. It felt like a time when anything was possible. The last two Christmases had certainly proven that to be true, and she was looking forward to seeing what this one held. Right now, it held the promise of a warm, cozy afternoon with her family, and hopefully some of her mother's peppermint bark. Her pregnancy cravings had largely involved sweets.

The inn was surprisingly quiet when she walked in. It was booked out for the season, another successful November and beginning of December so far, just like last year had been. When she'd come back home after a particularly bad breakup, taking a hiatus from her job in Boston as an event planner, she'd turned her attention on the local festival. Over the course of helping with it, she'd also come up with a business plan for the inn, which had been struggling that year. Her sister Caroline, and their parents Rhonda and Donovan, had taken her idea and run with it. Ever since, the inn's business had bounced back, and shown no signs of slowing down again. But this time of day, in the late afternoon, all of the guests were out and about. She saw one woman sitting by the fireplace, ensconced in a book with a cup of cocoa next to her, Rhonda's signature fluffy homemade marshmallows floating on top. The woman was so engrossed that she didn't even hear her walk in, and Nora slipped right on by, walking to the kitchen where she could smell the scent of muffins baking.

She found Rhonda and Caroline both in the kitchen. Rhonda was at the counter, stirring a bowl of something, and Caroline was leaning against it a little further down. But instead of the happy expressions Nora had been anticipating, they both wore pensive expressions that looked a little worried.

"Is everything okay?" Nora frowned, taking off her coat and scarf and draping them over the back of a chair before sitting down. She knew if she stood up for too long, Rhonda would start fussing over her. Her mother was thrilled to have a grandchild on the way, and was equally insistent that Nora shouldn't put herself out in the slightest.

Rhonda paused, glancing at Caroline before looking over at Nora. Nora felt a slight queasiness, wondering what was going on. She hadn't seen either of them look so worried since the inn hadn't been doing well.

"Margo is coming for a short visit," Rhonda said finally. "She'll be here tomorrow morning. She said she was driving down."

Nora blinked, caught completely by surprise. It was the last thing she'd ever expected her mother to say. None of them had heard from Margo in months, not since a quick call to check-in that had clearly been hurried on her end. They'd all agreed afterward that it had felt like Margo had something more important to do, and it had hurt all of their feelings a little, but Rhonda's especially. Nora privately had thought that Caroline had been hurt too, but she was better at hiding it.

She wasn't sure how to feel about Margo coming home. If phone calls had been sporadic, visits had been non-existent. She knew she didn't have a lot of room to talk. For years, she hadn't managed to make time to visit either. She'd been so caught up in her own life and the rat race of Boston that she'd kept pushing it off again and again until finally, it felt like she'd been gone so long that it was easier to just not visit. But deep down, she'd felt bad about it.

She didn't know if Margo *did* feel bad about how long it had been. Nora had always thought that Margo just felt that everything she had going on was more important, more exciting, and just overall more interesting than whatever Evergreen Hollow could hold. And while Nora could understand that feeling, she wasn't sure what reason there could be for Margo to come and visit now. It definitely wasn't that she'd suddenly found her Christmas spirit, and felt a deep need to come home for the holidays.

It didn't even sound as if she'd be staying for Christmas.

Caroline let out a soft sigh, and Nora could imagine what her older sister was thinking. She knew Caroline had often felt, over the years before Nora had come back and they'd made up, that she was the only sister who had ever helped their parents out. Unlike Nora and Margo, Caroline had stayed in Evergreen Hollow her whole life, helping Rhonda and Donovan run the inn. Since Nora had come home two years ago, she and Caroline had worked through a lot of those feelings together. But Nora knew there was a bit of residual resentment in

Caroline about how thoroughly Margo seemed to avoid the family, and she could feel the awkwardness radiating off Caroline as she stood there.

"How long is she coming for?" Nora asked, glancing at Caroline and then back at their mother.

"She didn't say exactly. Just a 'short visit'." Rhonda frowned. "I'm excited to see her, of course. I miss her."

There was an unspoken *but* that Nora could hear all the same. She knew her mother was concerned about how the three of them might get along, with Margo back after so long. It was probably made worse, she thought, by the fact that Margo was now the only one who hadn't come back to Evergreen Hollow. Once upon a time, she and Margo had at least had their absence from their childhood home in common. But now, she had a feeling that Margo was going to feel like the odd one out, the only remaining prodigal daughter.

It was a recipe for an interesting family reunion, that was for sure. And she wasn't certain how it would all play out.

"Don't worry." Nora smiled at her mother, trying to sound reassuring. "It'll be a good thing, having Margo here for a little of the holidays. We all haven't seen her in so long."

She thought she sounded convincing enough. But inwardly, she wasn't so sure. Even just for herself, she already felt so emotional from dealing with the pregnancy, and all of the changes it had brought along with it. As excited as she was, it was a lot to deal with.

And now, this just felt like another uncertainty to try and handle.

CHAPTER FOUR

For the first time in years, Margo turned into the driveway of The Mistletoe Inn.

The drive had been fine. Once again, her trusty Subaru had gotten her from Jersey to her destination —in this case, Vermont—with no trouble at all. Her mother had seemed surprised that she wasn't flying, but she'd actually been looking forward to the drive. It had felt like a good opportunity to get her thoughts in order, and mentally prepare herself to go home and see her family for the first time in so long. The short flight, she thought, wouldn't have been enough.

The inn looked just as she remembered it. It had snowed, giving the entire place a cozy, picturesque look that would have fit perfectly on a Christmas card. It was fully decorated outside for the holidays, with lights strung across the wraparound porch, garlands around the stairs and railing, reindeer in the snow, and a snowman. Inside was probably decorated to the nines as well, Margo thought as she turned off the car, glimpsing the twinkle of lights from a tree near one of the large windows. Her mother had always decorated as soon as the Thanksgiving holidays were over, and she wasn't at all surprised to find that Rhonda was sticking with that tradition.

It *was* beautiful. She could admit that, even if she was already beginning to feel her stomach knot with anxiety at the idea of being home again. The inn looked cozy and rustic, and everything that a Vermont cabin at Christmastime should be.

She jumped a little as the front door opened, letting out a warm glow of buttery light, and her mother stepped out onto the porch.

Margo swallowed hard, and got out of the car.

"You're here!" Rhonda called out, starting toward the steps. Margo almost called out for her to wait—she knew her mother had had a hip replacement several years ago, and she worried about her on the potentially icy stairs—but Rhonda was already halfway down them before Margo could say anything. "How was the drive?"

"Not bad." Margo swallowed again, past the sudden lump in her throat, and walked toward her mother to give her a quick hug. Rhonda, at least, looked happy to see her. She didn't see any sign of Caroline, but she knew her older sister couldn't be far off. Caroline didn't take days off from the inn, which meant she was somewhere handling some aspect of it.

Or maybe not. She remembered coming home earlier in the year to a wedding invitation for Caroline. She'd been shocked that her sister had met someone. She remembered Caroline as always being wholly uninterested in dating, completely caught up in the inn and her responsibilities. Married to it, really, for all intents and purposes.

But according to the invite that Margo had gotten, Caroline had met an absolutely gorgeous man and gotten engaged in a bit of a whirlwind relationship. The second of her sisters to do so, actually.

She'd been home when Nora's wedding invitation had come in the mail the year before that, but she'd had an assignment in Madrid that weekend, a full two months that she was supposed to be in Spain. So she'd had to send her apologies, and tell Nora she was excited to see pictures. She'd seen *tons* of photos from Nora's wedding on her sister's Instagram page. Moving back home hadn't affected Nora's affinity for carefully curated social media spaces at all. But Caroline still had a flip phone, if Margo remembered correctly. So she had no idea what that wedding had been like.

Still, she'd missed both of them. Another mark against her, even if both times had been for work. And it occurred to her that Caroline, for the first time, might not be bustling around the inn. Surely she lived somewhere else now, and hadn't just moved her new husband in.

"It's freezing." Rhonda squeezed her daughter tightly again, jolting Margo out of her thoughts. "Grab your bags, and come in. I just took a pecan pie out of the oven, and I'll put some coffee on."

"Pie?" Margo raised an eyebrow. "It's nine in the morning, Mom."

"That's not too early for pie. I was up at five baking anyway. These last two seasons the inn has been absolutely *packed*—thanks to Nora, by the way, and Caroline executing her plan *so* well—and now that Caroline doesn't live at home anymore, I've had to be on top of the baking. Can't have the guests missing out." Rhonda beamed, and Margo forced a smile.

Well, that answered her question about
Caroline's new living arrangements, at least.

"I'll get my things." She went around to the back
of the car, opening the hatch and using it as an
opportunity to gather herself. She'd always thought
of Evergreen Hollow as a sleepy, slow-moving place,
frozen in time. In many ways, it had been, and she
imagined it still was. But there were clearly parts of
life that were moving along just fine, and she was
suddenly struck with how much she'd missed. She'd
had the idea that she would come home and
everything would be just as she left it, but that
clearly wasn't true.

Nora had come home and apparently re-
integrated herself into the family so smoothly that
she was helping with the inn now too. It sounded like
there had been a lull in business that she'd helped
reinvigorate. And both Margo's sisters were married.
Caroline had found her own sense of purpose
outside of the inn.

Just when her own life had come to a sudden,
shrieking halt, everyone else appeared to be moving
along just fine. She felt that knot of anxiety in her
stomach tighten, anticipating the potential of pity
from her sisters. She had always been the one with
the exciting, globe-trotting life. Now she was

crawling home with her tail between her legs, and the last thing she wanted was to be the object of her family's pity.

Letting out a sharp sigh, her breath puffing in the air in front of her, Margo slung her duffel bag over her shoulder and followed her mother inside.

The moment she stepped into the living room, she was instantly struck with a sense of déjà vu, wrapped in an aching feeling of nostalgia that she hadn't had in a long time. The room smelled of cinnamon and the faint, sugary scents of baked goods, a whiff of ham and egg quiche mixed in.

The living room was bright with Christmas decorations, exactly as she had expected, and she heard the chatter of guests from the dining room, having their breakfast. A quick glance past the open wood-and-glass double doors that led into the room told her that Rhonda had been right about the inn being packed. Every seat at the long dining table was full.

She wasn't surprised to hear that Nora had come up with a business plan to help the inn. Her business acumen had always been good, and combined with Caroline's steadfast dedication to making sure The Mistletoe Inn endured over the years, they would likely be unstoppable.

She felt another small twist in her chest, realizing how much had happened while she'd been gone.

"Here." Rhonda led Margo into the kitchen, which smelled warmly of muffins, pie, and the breakfast quiche. "Just set your bag down there for now. I'll get the coffee on, and then we'll get you settled in after your sisters get here. I'm sure they're excited to see you."

She felt a quiver of anxiety at that. She wasn't nearly as certain. "I can always get a room somewhere the next town over, if you're too full here," Margo offered. "I don't want to take up space that someone could be paying for."

"Nonsense." Rhonda shook her head, pouring coffee grounds into a filter. "Caroline's room has been empty ever since she moved out. I thought about converting it into another guest room, but it's just down the hall from your father's and my room, and that's a little closer than I like guests to be. So we haven't decided just yet. It's a perfectly good extra room for you to stay in when you come to visit."

Margo couldn't help hearing the pointed note in her mother's voice, which sounded very much like a suggestion that, now that she'd finally made the trek home, maybe she would find it within herself to do so more often. But she didn't want to make any promises just yet. It all felt too uncertain, like poking at a bruise to see just how deep it went.

Silence fell over the kitchen for several long minutes while Rhonda made coffee, and Margo shifted uneasily in her chair, glancing out the window. For all that things had definitely changed since she'd been home last, some things had also very much stayed the same. The kitchen, and all its furnishings and dishes, was exactly as she remembered it. The view out of the window by the small breakfast nook was the same, looking out at the snowy backyard and the maples in the distance, the pens with the chickens and goats just off to the right. There was a small, roped-off area with a sign that Margo didn't remember, and she frowned.

"What's that? Are you building a new enclosure for animals or something?"

Rhonda glanced out of the window in the direction Margo was pointing as she poured the coffee, and laughed. "Oh, no," she said, setting down the mugs and going to the refrigerator for creamer. "Caroline's stepson has a bit of an obsession with fossils. Someone put it into his head that there are some buried in our backyard. So Caroline roped off a 'dig site' for him, so he'd have his own space to play in and not put holes all over the yard."

Margo couldn't help the way her brows shot up at that. She'd never imagined her sister having any patience with children, especially not a little terror who ran around digging up Caroline's carefully tended backyard. Margo couldn't picture Caroline having patience with *anyone* who damaged the inn or its grounds in any way.

Rhonda chuckled again, clearly seeing Margo's expression as she brought the coffee, creamer, and two slices of pecan pie to the table. "I know what you're thinking. But Caroline really has softened up a lot. Nora coming home helped. And then after she met Rhett and Jay..." Rhonda shrugged, a soft smile on her face. "She's really grown into being a wife and stepmother. I think it's good for her, having something that matters outside of this place. It's helped her a lot."

Margo nodded, once again feeling that lump in her throat. She reached for the creamer, pouring several slugs of it into her coffee until it was a light tan, and handed it back to her mother, who smiled indulgently at her.

"You always did like a little coffee with your creamer."

Margo tried to force a smile back onto her face, but it was hard. She felt out of place, uncertain, and she wondered if this had been a good idea at all.

Maybe she should have just taken off to California for a few weeks, gotten some sun. A flight to Mexico, maybe. But her savings weren't *that* prolific, and she'd known coming home was a better move until she had a plan. She'd always focused on living in the moment, enjoying every possible experience while she was on location for work, and she didn't regret it. But it did mean that she didn't have the nest egg she probably should have.

"So." Rhonda cut a bite of pie. "What happened with the magazine?"

"I didn't get fired." The words came out faster than she could think, and more defensive than she meant for them to, a knee-jerk reaction that she couldn't stop. But it felt so sensitive. She'd worked so hard, and hadn't done anything wrong—even Richard had made that clear. But she'd lost the job anyway.

Gently, Rhonda placed a hand over hers. "I wasn't thinking that at all, sweetheart," she said calmly. "I just wanted to know what happened, that's all. I know how devoted you were to that job."

Margo nodded, biting her lip. "I'm sorry. I'm a

little on edge about seeing Nora and Caroline again, I think," she admitted. "I feel like they're going to hold how long it's been against me. I know I haven't talked to anyone that much."

Rhonda let out a soft sigh. "Just give it time," she advised. "They might be a bit on edge too. But everything will smooth over soon enough, once things settle down. You coming home out of the blue was a surprise to everyone. A good one," she added quickly. "But let them adjust a little to you being here again."

Margo let out a breath, taking a bite of the pie. It was just as good as she remembered, crunchy pecans and the sweet, sticky pie beneath, with the flaky crust that only her mother could make. It went perfectly with the coffee and the cinnamon creamer, and she had to admit that pie for breakfast wasn't really a bad idea at all.

"I wasn't fired," she repeated. "I was laid off."

"Why?" Rhonda sat back, sipping her coffee. "Company problems?"

Margo nodded. "I guess it had been going on for a while, I just didn't pay enough attention. Or take it seriously enough, I guess. I was in Egypt, doing a piece, and I saw some comments in the work chat, a few emails I don't think I was really supposed to be a part of. If I'd looked at it more, I probably wouldn't have been so blindsided. But I'd come back home, figuring it was all fine, with a new pitch for my boss and plans of being in the Caribbean on assignment for Christmas. Turns out, they had budget cuts and I was one of the ones being let go."

"That's not your fault," Rhonda said reassuringly. "You couldn't do anything about that."

"I know." Margo stabbed at the pie with her fork, scooping up another bite. "It doesn't make it feel better though. I loved that job. And actual magazine jobs are getting harder and harder to come by. It's not going to be easy, replacing it. I might have to do something else for a while."

She felt her chest tighten at the thought, disappointment and a faint sense of dread flooding through her all over again. Both feelings had been lingering beneath the surface ever since Richard had given her the news, ready to crop up at any moment. "This is just going to be for a few days," she said, looking up at her mother. "Just while I think about what my next move is."

"You can stay as long as you—oh, there are your sisters." Rhonda stood up, flashing Margo a reassuring smile before going to meet Nora and Caroline in the living room.

Margo tensed, setting her fork down as she heard footsteps approaching. But every other thought fled from her mind as Nora and Caroline walked in, and she saw Nora's bump.

"What?" She exclaimed before she could stop herself, staring wide-eyed at Nora. "I—I—how did I not know about something this important? You're *pregnant*?"

"I am," Nora said wryly, but Caroline broke in before Nora could say anything else.

"Well, we haven't heard from you in six months." She shrugged. "It would've been hard to tell you about something that I didn't even know about yet the last time we talked."

It was impossible to miss the bite in her voice. Margo winced, and Rhonda immediately interrupted.

"I have pecan pie. Margo already has a piece, does anyone else want one?"

"Sure." Nora sank down into a chair, Caroline following suit as she accepted the offer too. But it was very clear, Margo thought, that no one was actually thinking about pie.

Caroline looked exactly as she remembered. Dark hair with a smattering of grays pulled back into a low ponytail, no-nonsense jeans and a flannel shirt buttoned over a plain t-shirt.

Nora, on the other hand, was still sleek and put-together, but much more dressed-down compared to the designer-wear business casual that Margo remembered from the last time she'd seen her sister. Nora was wearing skinny jeans and a long red cable-knit sweater, her hair up in a messy bun and not a speck of makeup. She still looked flawless—it was innate for her, Margo thought—but she looked like she belonged in the picturesque coziness of Evergreen Hollow, not in the fast-paced world of Boston any longer.

Margo was the only one, it seemed, who felt out of place.

"So, what's the plan?" Caroline asked, looking at Margo. "Mom said something about the magazine letting you go."

Margo bit back her instant defensive response. "Laid off," she said, still a little more curtly than she meant to. "Budget cuts. Figuring out a plan is why I came here for a few days. I thought it was as good a time as any to take advantage of the chance to come home, and decide what to do next."

Caroline made a small *hm* sound, and Margo bit her lip. Caroline hadn't said anything outwardly disapproving, but she thought she could practically *feel* it wafting off her, and Nora hadn't said anything at all.

It felt like there was a clear disconnect among all of them, and no one quite knew what to say. The silence hung heavy and awkward in the air as Rhonda brought the slices of pie, sitting back down at the table with her daughters.

"Does anyone want to fill me in on what's been going on around Evergreen Hollow?" Margo asked, just to break the tension. "I'm so sorry I missed your weddings. Work was really busy, and the assignments were very demanding, so I couldn't get away. But I wish I could've been there to celebrate with you."

She paused, sure that she could hear the unspoken thoughts in the air. *You missed these important events, and what good did it do you anyway? You still lost your job.*

"It's okay," Nora said quietly. "We understand. But you were definitely missed, I can tell you that."

Margo nodded, biting her lip. "So, catch me up on what else I missed. What have you both been up to?"

Nora smiled, cutting into her piece of pie, and began to regale Margo with a story from last

Christmas, telling her about the house she'd bought with Aidan just after they were married and an apparent kerfuffle involving a chandelier.

Margo listened, a little stunned as her sister went on about the difficulties of getting an Art Deco chandelier shipped to Evergreen Hollow, and how the community had ended up donating a bunch of glass trinkets to handmake a chandelier before Nora's Christmas party instead. And she told it, Margo realized, with the same enthusiasm that she'd once heard her sister describe successfully pulling off an event for a billionaire's daughter's sweet sixteen.

It was, apparently, a perfect segue for Nora and their mother to tell Margo about Caroline's whirlwind romance, which had been started by a faulty smoke detector that had ended up being caused by a poorly wired faux fireplace. Margo nodded along, taking bites of her pie, feeling slightly shell-shocked.

They were telling the stories as if there was nothing odd about it. As if it were all *exciting*. She could understand some of it, coming from Caroline— after all, bad smoke detectors and a handsome firefighter probably *was* the most exciting thing that had happened to Caroline in years. But she couldn't grasp how Nora had changed so much. It made her feel even more out of place, seeing her once elegant and ambitious sister now thrilled about a DIY chandelier.

She wanted more than anything to feel at home again. She'd hoped that she might be able to. But she couldn't understand why they were all so happy and content with lives that, to her, seemed so awfully drab.

Margo finished the pie, just as Rhonda started to ask Nora questions about nursery wallpaper. She couldn't stand it any longer, she thought. The kitchen felt small and hot, and her family overwhelming. She needed some fresh air.

"I'm going to go for a walk," she said, standing up and forcing a smile onto her face. "See the sights a little. It's such a pretty day, and it's been so long, you know?"

She didn't think anyone was fooled, but she also couldn't bring herself to care. She grabbed her coat, throwing it on over her sweater, and fled out the back door of the kitchen.

The cold air hit her like a slap in the face after the warmth of the inside of the inn, but she sucked in a deep breath of it, relishing the sting for a moment. She started to walk, wanting to put as much distance as she could between herself and all the feelings that being back in that kitchen with her family had dredged up.

How am I going to survive a few days here?

She'd been hopeful that it wouldn't be so bad, but she already felt trapped. She couldn't fathom how Nora had apparently settled in here so easily, already married with a house and a baby on the way. It wasn't all that long ago that she remembered Nora being engaged to someone else, a longtime boyfriend in Boston. She wondered what had happened there.

But of course, she didn't know. And if she asked, someone—probably Caroline—would point out that it was her fault, for not calling more often and never visiting.

She needed *something* to keep herself occupied, or she was going to go insane.

Margo kept walking, trying to focus on the feeling of the cold air in her lungs and the crunch of snow under her boots, trying to ground herself. And then she saw a large wooden sign and looked up, the bright lettering catching her eye.

Maple Trail Skiing! Open for the season!

She hadn't been skiing in a long time. Truthfully, she wasn't at all sure she remembered how. But she immediately decided that tomorrow, that would be what she'd devote her day to doing. Something else to focus on, and physical exercise at that, as well as something to do *away* from the inn.

That, she thought, should clear her mind enough to decide what to do next.

* * *

Spencer stepped out of Rockridge Grill, breathing in deeply as he tucked in his scarf. Another perk of the small-town doctor life, not only regular lunch breaks, he thought, but also the ability to get a decent breakfast before his first appointment of the day. Gone were the days of scarfing down a dry muffin and a paper cup of black cafeteria coffee. Instead, he got to start his day with a fresh cup topped off with local creamer, and a hearty omelet. He'd have more energy and better focus, and he definitely enjoyed his days more.

There was the added perk of being close friends with the owner and chef at Rockridge Grill, Jonathan Keller. They'd hit it off almost as soon as Spencer had moved home, and he always enjoyed chatting with Jonathan whenever he came by to eat. It made for a relaxing way to start the morning whenever he didn't have an early appointment; a good breakfast and good conversation with a friend.

As he turned to start walking toward the clinic, he spotted someone he didn't recognize standing next to the skiing sign, looking intently at it. A woman, he saw, who looked very purposeful in the way she was staring at the sign, as if it held some answer she'd been looking for.

She was also very beautiful, Spencer thought. Dark brown hair that she'd braided into buns at the back of her head, and big, wide blue eyes taking in that sign, wrapped up in a cozy-looking sweater and jeans. Someone he definitely would have noticed, if she'd been around prior to this.

Probably a tourist, only here for a few days. But, as he continued on his way, he couldn't help wondering who she was.

CHAPTER FIVE

"Oh, boy." Nora let out a long breath as she set the boxes that had come in the mail down on the coffee table in her living room, marveling at how much harder it was to carry literally anything at five months pregnant. Above her, the chandelier that was her pride and joy twinkled in the morning light spilling through the large bay window of the living room. She looked up at it, smiling at the memory of how everyone in the community had come together last Christmas to help her salvage her dream of the perfect centerpiece for her Victorian Christmas party.

Margo had looked decidedly unimpressed by the story. Nora knew her sister was probably reeling at the change in her especially. But Rhonda seemed sure that she'd come around, that she just needed a few days to adjust to being back home. Problem was, Nora thought, Margo seemed to plan on only being in town for a few days. She wasn't going to settle in, she was going to detonate, and then disappear again.

Letting out a breath, Nora opened the first box, smiling down at the neatly folded blankets in pastel pinks and greens made of a soft fabric. She reached in to touch one of them, still feeling slightly as if she was in a dream. She could still hardly believe that in a few months, she'd be a mother to a baby girl.

It didn't feel quite real. She wasn't sure it *would* feel real until she actually had her baby in her arms.

She set the box aside, nudging a few magazines to one side of the glossy dark-wood coffee table. The living room was her favorite spot in the house, and she'd taken special care decorating it, just as she had the rest of the old Victorian that she and Aiden had bought.

Everything here, from the coffee table with its curved antique legs, to the forest green velvet sofa and brocade throw pillows, and the thick tapestried rug in the middle of the floor, she'd picked out with an eye for playing up the historic features of the room. It had gorgeous windows and vaulted ceilings, and she couldn't wait to decorate for Christmas again. The nook in the window had stacks of old books artfully placed in it now, and she'd found the perfect old-fashioned lamps to set next to them and light up at night with votive candles.

Shaking her head, she pulled herself back to the moment, and went to carry the first box up to the nursery. Aiden would probably have something to say about it when he got home for lunch, but she didn't want to always have to ask him for help.

She'd always been capable of handling things like boxes and decorating around the house, and she knew she was going to need help with the decorations this year, which already needled at her. She couldn't wait for the end result of the pregnancy, but it was a bit of a struggle in the meantime. Especially since the excitement that she often felt about what was ahead of them changed to nervousness when she was alone, and could get in her head about what could possibly go wrong.

She focused on unpacking the boxes instead once she had them upstairs in the nursery, setting the folded blankets on the maple wood dresser and taking the swatches of wallpaper out of the envelope they'd been sent in. She had a handful of tacks, and started lining them up on one wall, pursing her lips as she considered which one she liked best. They'd already settled on blush pink and mint green for the nursery, so she thought a neutral color might be best—

There was a light knock against the doorjamb, and Nora jumped a little, turning to see Aiden standing there. He was wearing jeans and a wool sweater with the sleeves pushed up to his elbows, and she thought she saw a little bit of wood shavings caught in his hair. He looked as handsome as always, especially when he smiled at her.

"I knocked so I *wouldn't* startle you," he said with a laugh, walking in to stand behind her and wrap his arms around her waist. "What are you up to?"

"Nothing much." Nora gestured at the wall. "Trying to decide on wallpaper. Or paint. Maybe just painting it would be better."

Aiden grinned. "Isn't wallpaper easier to swap out when you get a different decorating idea in six months?"

Nora swatted his arm, but she laughed. "You're right, wallpaper is probably the better idea."

Aiden rested his chin atop her head, looking at the boxes scattered around the room. "How did things go with your sister?"

Nora sighed, extricating herself from his arms

and walking over to the pile of folded blankets, toying with one satin edge. "It's a little strange having her back," she admitted. "It's just a weird time. I already feel out of whack from the pregnancy, and the holidays are always a little chaotic. Having Margo here just adds another layer of stress. It wouldn't if I thought she was happy to be here, but she doesn't seem to be. It seems more like she just needed an inexpensive place to get her bearings and thought crashing at the inn was her best option."

"You weren't all that thrilled to be here at first when you came back," Aiden reminded her gently. "I think you had some pretty rough moments too, as I recall. Just be patient with her."

"I know. Mom said the same thing."

Aiden chuckled. "Far be it from me to disagree with your mother."

"At least I planned on staying for the holiday when I came home." Nora pursed her lips. "Margo said a few days, maybe. She's just planning to blow in and back out, I guess. She stays longer on location for work than she ever has at home."

"But she lost that job, right?" Aiden crossed his arms, considering. "It might take her a minute to get back on her feet. She might decide to do that here. And that would be a good thing, wouldn't it?"

"Maybe." Nora considered. "I don't want to be too hard on her. After all, I stayed away from home for a long time too. But I also don't want her to stress Mom out. You know how she is. She hasn't seen Margo in so long, and she's going to want to make everything okay."

"Maybe it will be." Aiden gave her a reassuring smile. "Anyway, you can't control what everyone does. Margo will go her own way, if what you've said is any indication, and nothing is going to change that. So just focus on what you can control."

Nora laughed. "You're right. Wallpaper swatches are much easier to deal with than Margo."

As if on cue, her phone rang. She dug it out of her pocket, half-expecting it to be a client with last-minute holiday requests, but she saw her mother's name on the screen. She quickly answered it, mouthing *just a second* to Aiden.

"Mom?"

"Nora. Can you come over? Caroline said she would be here in a minute, but I need help. There's a huge leak in the ceiling of the inn, and after that snow we just had, I'm a little worried."

"Oh no! Yeah, of course, I'll be right there. Give me a few minutes."

Nora hung up the phone, feeling her stomach

sink as she looked at Aiden. It was the worst possible timing, of course. Right in the middle of the holiday season, and with Margo home on top of it.

When it rains, it pours.

She let out a sigh, looking at her husband. "Can you drive me over to the inn? There's an emergency."

Margo stared up at the spreading stain on the roof, forcing herself to bite back a sharp sigh of frustration.

She'd planned to already be out of the inn and on the ski slopes. It was impossible to get up earlier than her mother, but she'd hoped she could use the guests' breakfast hour as a distraction, grab a pumpkin cream cheese muffin and coffee to-go, and get out of the inn as quickly as possible. But, of course, that hadn't worked out the way she'd hoped.

First, she'd gotten a call about a mix-up with her apartment. It happened more often than she liked since she was home so rarely. A leasing agent would think it was one available to show, or the maintenance guy would get the wrong door number, or they would need to do a walkthrough and get her permission since she wasn't home. She'd gotten used to it as just one of the slight annoyances of a job that kept her on the go, but now it was both one more thing she didn't want to deal with, and also a reminder that she no longer had the excuse of work to be away.

Now, it was just that she didn't want to be there.

She'd only just gotten that ironed out and managed to jump in and out of the shower and get dressed when she'd gotten a second phone call, this one from her bank. She'd lost a credit card while she was in Egypt, and since the card had been lost out of the country, there were more hoops to jump through than just the usual rigmarole of getting it canceled and a new one sent out. Then, once she'd straightened out the issues of the lost card, she'd had to give them the inn's address to send the new card to —before remembering that she'd only planned to stay here for a few days, and the card would probably show up after she'd left.

It's fine, she'd decided frustratedly after hanging up the phone. *I'll just ask Mom to forward it to me if that happens. I have other cards.* She only had one other card though, now that her company one was gone, and her debit. She was okay on money for now, but it wouldn't last her long. Skiing was probably an unnecessary expense, but she decided she was chalking it up to her mental health. If only her insurance would cover it—

That was a reminder that she wouldn't have that in a month either. The stresses of the morning had felt like they were piling in on her until she wanted to scream, but she'd hung up the phone and told herself that it was fine, that she was going to grab breakfast and coffee, and head out.

And then the inn's roof sprang a leak, and there was no quietly escaping the house. Especially since Rhonda had needed input from the entire family about what to do, and now both Margo's sisters and their respective husbands were crowded around, along with Rhonda and Donovan, looking at the roof as if it would give them an answer.

"Well, I can probably do something about it," Aiden said, rubbing a hand over his mouth. "Wouldn't be the first roof I worked on in Evergreen Hollow." He chuckled, and Margo saw a faint smile cross Nora's face. It stung a little, because there was clearly an inside joke there that she didn't understand, a reference to some past moment that she hadn't been a part of. She had to remind herself that she'd willingly excluded herself from all of that, that it had been her choice to pursue a career that kept her away. But it still hurt, and she bit her lip, feeling a twinge of regret.

"You have all those other jobs though," Rhonda protested. "I don't want to keep you away from the people who have already contracted you."

"Winter isn't all that busy when there's not a rogue storm blowing through. Besides, who else is going to do it? Leon?" Aiden chuckled. "He's getting a bit old to be climbing on roofs."

"Not to mention, we all know what happened when he hooked up Caroline's fireplace," Rhett chimed in, and Caroline laughed. It startled Margo. She couldn't remember the last time she'd heard her older sister *laugh* like that. In whatever way meeting this firefighter had changed her, it had clearly made her happier. Margo looked at him curiously. He was handsome, for sure. She was curious about what *had* happened, because that one comment had Caroline giving him a look of such happy adoration that Margo couldn't believe it was her sister looking at a man like that.

There would be time to find out all of those things, if you stayed for longer. She shook her head, stepping away from the others, who were still discussing how much of Aiden's time it would take up to repair the leak. Rhonda was insisting he should invoice the inn, and Aiden was arguing that as her son-in-law, he should just do it.

Margo rubbed her temples, glancing at the front door. If she snuck out now, she could probably escape. But just as she started to move further away from the group, toward the front door and her freedom on the ski slopes, her phone started buzzing again.

She dug it out of her pocket, looking at the name on the screen. It was the bank, probably calling with more issues involving her lost card.

She sighed, answering it. *So much for skiing.*

CHAPTER SIX

By the time she did finally make it to the ski slope, she was ridiculously late.

"It's going to get dark soon," the woman running the check-in desk told her, glancing out at the late-afternoon skies. "We normally don't let anyone head out at this time of day. It's not really advised."

Margo blew out a sharp breath. "I know. I grew up here. I'm just back in town for a few days, and I'd really like to get a look at the slopes. I'll be careful."

The woman didn't look convinced, and Margo tried to hold back her irritation. The woman was just doing her job, but *everything* had gone wrong so far that day, and she wasn't sure she could handle one more thing. She needed something to go *right*.

"I spent my whole life until I was eighteen in

Evergreen Hollow. I know it like the back of my hand, including when it gets dark. I'll be fine."

"What's your name?" The woman looked at her quizzically.

"Margo Stoker."

"*Oh.* Stoker. Your mom runs the inn." The woman relaxed a fraction as she said it, and Margo knew she'd won, but it didn't make her feel as good as she would have thought. Of course no one really remembered her, even Nora had been back home more than Margo had. But she got that sharp, pained feeling again, realizing how disconnected she really was from everything. She'd gotten what she wanted, getting away from home and severing almost all of her ties, but it didn't feel good, now that she was back.

"All right." The woman pushed paperwork toward her. "A liability statement, all the usual stuff. You sign this, and you'll be good to go."

Margo scribbled her name in the highlighted spots, and pushed the papers back toward the woman. "Okay. Here you are."

The cold air struck her again as she walked back out of the small building. It was getting colder, as it got closer to sunset, and she tucked her scarf a little closer around her neck, tugging her beanie down around her ears. There was still plenty of light out, she thought, and she collected her skis and poles, heading out toward the slopes.

She just wanted to get away for a little while. Some time to think. She'd thought being back at the inn would give her that, but it had turned out to be more confusing than anything else.

It did help, a little. Part of what she'd always loved about her job was the ability to explore, to go places and document the world around her, and the freedom of being out on the ski slopes helped to give her back some of that feeling. There weren't very many people left out there, most of them had already headed back, and as she ventured further she realized soon that she was the only one left skiing. She didn't mind it.

But she also realized that it was getting dark faster than she had thought it would. It had snuck up on her, and she took a deep breath, realizing it was time to head back. It had probably been time twenty minutes ago. Now, it would be full dark before she made it back to the top.

She was good at this though, she reminded herself. She was good at navigating difficult situations and staying calm. She just needed to remember that, and she would get through this.

Carefully, she started to navigate her way back, peering upward in the gathering twilight. She was halfway up before she paused for a moment to catch her breath, trying to gauge how much further she had to go before it would be too dark to see at all.

Not far. She took another step—and felt her foot slip, unable to find purchase as it slid out from under her. She scrambled to try to catch herself, but it was already too late, and she let out an undignified scream as she started to fall back down the slope.

She felt every bump as she tumbled down, and then an awful, sharp pain shooting up her leg as she landed, her foot bent under her.

She didn't need to look down at it to know that her leg was broken.

"Help!" She shouted up the slopes, hoping that she hadn't stayed out so long that everyone had already gone home. But surely all of the employees wouldn't have left while there was still someone on the slopes who hadn't signed out yet.

A wave of relief washed over her as she saw two of the attendants, in their bright blue windbreakers and skis with the blue tape on the sides, start to head down the slope toward her.

"What's wrong?" They stopped on either side of Margo, and she gestured to her leg.

"I think it's broken." She swallowed back a gasp of pain. "I'm going to need help getting back up the slope. And maybe an ambulance to an emergency room."

"Radio up and tell someone to call Doctor Thorpe. We'll get you back into town, don't worry."

Who is Doctor Thorpe?

She didn't have much time to think about it, because the two attendants were helping her up, and all she could think about was the pain shooting through her leg.

They helped her back up the slopes, all the way to a waiting car, where one of the attendants held open the door and the other supported her while she slid inside, her mind racing. "We'll head into town now," the man getting into the driver's seat said, and Margo nodded numbly.

How could this happen?

All she'd wanted was to get a little time alone to clear her head, and things had gone from bad to worse. She'd felt confident that she would be fine out on the slopes, long enough to get back before it was completely dark. And yet somehow, things had gone from bad to worse so quickly.

She didn't even know if Evergreen Hollow *had* the means to treat a broken leg. She couldn't remember what the doctor's office in town was like, but she was pretty sure the doctor who ran it was ancient. It didn't instill a lot of confidence that they'd be able to help her, and she wished they'd just called an ambulance that could take her to Providence. She would have felt better about everything.

Briefly, she considered calling her mother and letting Rhonda know what had happened. But she didn't want to do that either. Rhonda would just worry, and the last thing Margo wanted was to give her mother something else to worry about, especially after what had happened with the roof this morning.

The medical office in town, she saw as the attendants driving her there pulled up in front of it, was a small white-sided building with a dark gray gabled roof, and matching shutters on the windows. It looked more like a home than a doctor's office, she thought, cozy and appealing, but not necessarily where she wanted to go for an injury like this. But it didn't seem like she was going to get much of a choice.

Despite the late hour, there was a nurse waiting when the ski attendants helped her hobble in, a dark-haired, middle-aged woman who introduced herself as Gemma.

"We'll just get you into an exam room," she said,

taking over from the attendants and thanking them. "And Doctor Thorpe will be in to see you in a few minutes."

Margo smiled tightly, wincing from the pain as the nurse got her situated in the exam room, helping her up onto a table and bustling around as she took Margo's temperature and blood pressure. Her leg was still shooting sparks of pain all the way up her side, and she closed her eyes for a moment, trying hard not to panic. She could see it swelling, and she didn't want to look at it any longer.

Gemma left, promising the wait wouldn't be long, and Margo opened her eyes again, staring up at the ceiling. She had no idea what on earth she was going to do. She needed to look for a new job, but she couldn't exactly go out on assignments with a broken leg, even if she managed to find a new position so quickly.

She either wouldn't get hired, or she would, and she'd start off her first months at a new magazine or paper chained to a desk, working on editing other people's articles and seeing all the far-flung, fantastic places they got to go. That sounded worse than being unemployed—other than the part where she wasn't getting paid at all right now.

Glancing around the room, she noticed with

surprise that there was a small tapestry on the opposing wall. Not at all what she would expect to see in a doctor's office, and she peered a little more closely at it, realizing that it was an authentic Indian mandala. That surprised her too. It wasn't just some knock-off, whoever had hung it there had clearly traveled.

There was an elephant in the center of it, she saw. And then, she noticed the tapestry was lagging on one side. It was turning the elephant's trunk downward, and that was bad luck. It needed to always be pointing up, toward the sky.

She knew she should leave it alone. Focus on the bigger problems she had right now.

It's just a tapestry, she told herself. *It doesn't really matter*.

But it was bothering her, and she wanted to fix it.

Frowning, she sat up, maneuvering herself off the exam table. She held on to the side of it with one hand, hopping toward the opposite wall, and tried to reach up with her free hand to fix the tapestry, but it was a little too high for her to reach.

She let out a frustrated breath, and moved a little closer. There was a table underneath it, and she tried to push herself up onto it, thinking she could reach higher from there.

Unfortunately, it was a rolling table, and the moment she tried to push herself onto it, it moved away from her.

She let out a yelp as she slipped, suddenly terrified that she was going to fall and injure herself even worse than before. She could feel herself about to fall—

—and then a pair of strong arms wrapped around her, keeping her from hitting the ground, and lifting her up so that she didn't have to put any weight on her injured leg.

Margo looked up to see one of the most handsome men she'd ever seen looking down at her. He had sandy blond hair, hazel eyes with just the right amount of green in them, and a strong, clean-shaven jaw. He was looking down at her, concerned, and for a moment she forgot about the pain in her leg.

"Are you all right?" He helped her back to the exam table, steadying her so that she could get back on it. "You're meant to stay here, you know." There was a hint of humor in his voice, so she could tell he wasn't annoyed.

"I—" She felt foolish now, explaining it. "I saw your tapestry. It's crooked on one side, so the elephant's trunk is pointing down." She gestured toward the tapestry. "It's bad luck if it's not upright all of the time."

The man's eyes sparkled with amusement as he shoved his hands in his pockets, giving her an appraising look. "A friend brought that for me as a gift," he said. "How do you know about what it means?"

"I've been to India for work. I'm a photojournalist, and I work for..."

She trailed off, realizing that she didn't, in fact, work for them any longer. She was unemployed, and she had no idea when she would get to do the job she loved again, in the capacity that she used to do it in.

Especially now that she'd been reckless, and potentially badly hurt herself.

Her injured leg. That was why she was here, not to make small talk with a handsome man who had surprisingly good reflexes. She snapped back to reality, seeing that the man was still standing across from her, and studying her with a smile.

"Have you been here before?" she asked, feeling a tiny bit of annoyance creeping in. "I know it's late, but I feel like I've been waiting a long time, considering this is an emergency. Does it always take so long?"

The man chuckled. "I'm sorry I kept you

waiting, Ms. Stoker. Doctor Spencer Thorpe, at your service."

Margo blinked in surprise, staring at him. She'd expected the doctor to be an old, weathered man. She definitely hadn't expected—this.

What was such an attractive, young doctor doing in Evergreen Hollow?

"Can you tell me what happened?" Spencer stepped toward the table, gesturing for her to lie back as he tugged up the torn leg of her jeans. "I heard the employees from the ski slopes brought you in."

Margo nodded. "I just needed to get out and get some fresh air for a bit. So I went to check out the ski place, and they said it was getting late, but I figured as long as I didn't stay out too late it would be fine. But then it got dark faster than I expected, and I slipped, and—" She bit her lip, suddenly feeling as if all of it sounded ridiculous. "I think it's broken."

"It definitely looks like it," Spencer said sympathetically. "It's not an uncommon injury, out there on the slopes. Happens all the time."

"I feel like an idiot," she moaned, wincing as he touched her leg, examining the break. "I should have known better."

"Not at all," he assured her. "It can really sneak up on you, this time of year. Gets dark faster than you expect. And even experienced skiers can have an accident."

"I should have listened when they told me it was getting too late to go out," she mumbled, staring up at the ceiling. What was she going to do?

"Sometimes you just need some fresh air." Spencer smiled at her reassuringly, and Margo felt herself relax a little. Surprisingly, he was doing a remarkably good job at putting her at ease, despite the entire situation.

"Have you been here long?" she asked, changing the topic and trying to distract herself from the pain in her leg.

"About a year. I took over the practice when my father couldn't run it any longer. Can you move your toes?"

Margo tried and managed to produce a small wiggle. Spencer nodded, watching her closely.

"My guess is that it's a break," he told her. "We'll get you fitted with a brace for now, and if an x-ray shows that there's a fracture, you'll likely need a cast."

She felt a drop in her stomach at that, but it wasn't as dramatic as she would have thought. She couldn't believe how much better Spencer had made her feel, just chatting with her through the examination. He was definitely cut out to be a doctor, she thought, just as she looked up and saw Caroline and Nora walk in.

"How bad is it?" Nora asked, at the same time that Caroline spoke up.

"What were you thinking, Margo?"

She felt the small bubble of comfort around her instantly pop. She was pretty sure she knew exactly what they were thinking—that she had been reckless and impulsive, and what else should they have expected? Her life, to everyone in Evergreen Hollow, was unpredictable and chaotic, and she just *knew* they were judging her for doing something so irresponsible when her life was already coming apart at the seams.

"I thought it would be fine." She bit her lip. "I just needed to get out and work out some things. I obviously didn't think I'd break my leg."

"Of course not," Nora said soothingly, but Margo saw the look she exchanged with Caroline, one that was obviously worried, and Margo let out a long breath.

Nothing about this was going as planned.

* * *

Several days later, once the fracture had been confirmed by an x-ray and the swelling had gone down a bit, Margo sat in Doctor Thorpe's office again, feeling frustrated and helpless as he got her leg set in a cast and gave her a list of instructions.

Bed rest at first, no weight on it, no overdoing it.

Her frustration welled almost to a point of feeling like panic. In a matter of days, she'd gone from a globe-trotting job to now not being able to even go down a set of stairs without help. She felt trapped, and it didn't feel like a coincidence that something had happened to make her feel that way here in Evergreen Hollow.

"You ladies can get her home all right?" Spencer asked, glancing over at Nora and Caroline, who had accompanied Margo for her return visit. They both nodded. "All right. Take it easy," he warned Margo. "It's not too bad of a break, but it could be if you don't let it heal up right."

She nodded, sitting up and taking the paperwork he handed her. Despite the pain of her broken leg—thankfully numbed a bit by the painkillers he'd given her before setting it—and the overall awkwardness of the reason for her visit, she found herself wishing she could stay and talk with him for a little longer.

But what would be the point of that anyway? she

asked herself as she hobbled out to Nora's car, a new SUV that Nora had said she'd bought shortly after finding out she was pregnant.

There wasn't any reason to stay and chat up the town doctor, no matter how handsome he was.

She wasn't staying in Evergreen Hollow any longer than she had to.

CHAPTER SEVEN

Nora watched as Aiden came down from the ladder, a frown on his face. She was standing at the edge of the porch with her father, Donovan, waiting to hear what the diagnosis was on the leaky roof. From the expression on Aiden's face, she thought, it wasn't good news.

She waited until he had his feet on the ground before saying anything, her stomach knotting with worry. "Well? How bad is it?"

"Nothing you can't handle, right, son?" Donovan asked amiably, but Nora thought she could hear a hint of worry in her father's tone. The inn had been doing better the last couple of years, ever since she and Caroline had revamped the business plan together, but it wasn't so hugely profitable that they could go making big repairs without having to think twice about it. There was a lot of overhead that went with running a place like The Mistletoe Inn, and while Evergreen Hollow was popular with tourists, it wasn't exactly Newport.

Aiden let out a breath, running his hand through his hair. "It's pretty bad," he said reluctantly. "The whole roof is going to need to be repaired. Patching up that one leak is just going to spring another, and if there's a heavy snowfall come late December or January, like there usually is, I'm not sure it can handle it. I'd say you've been due a new roof for a few years now, looking at it, but it's hung in there. Now it really needs to be replaced." He frowned, letting out another heavy breath. "I hate to say it, but I'm going to need to hire some outside guys. Blake will help me, but this is more than a two-man job. Especially since we need to get it done fairly quickly, before there's any big snowfall."

Nora felt her blood pressure immediately spike, and she pressed a hand to the back of her neck, trying to calm down. It was the worst possible news. She knew her parents didn't have the kind of savings necessary to replace the whole roof. She and Aiden would have offered to help six months ago, but with the baby coming, things were tight for them too. And this was the slowest time of year for Aiden's construction work. Usually she had more events to handle for the holidays, but Aiden had urged her to slow down and enjoy her pregnancy, and she'd been happy to. But now she found herself wishing she'd kept working more, just so she could help her parents with this new stress.

"Well..." Donovan rubbed a hand over his beard. "We should probably go in and give your mother the news, hm?"

Nora knew under it all, he was just as stressed as the rest of them. He was just better at hiding it. He'd always been their mother's rock, and his daughters' too, when things were difficult. She was glad that she'd chosen to move back home to have a family. It felt good to be here, surrounded by them.

Even if it did feel like everything was happening at once. The usual chaos of the holidays, the baby, Margo coming home unexpectedly, and now this. It definitely wasn't the usual holiday season.

Rhonda was in the kitchen when the three of them walked in. Her face fell as soon as she turned around and saw the expressions on their faces. "Oh, it's not good, is it?"

Aiden let out another of those heavy sighs, as he explained the situation to her. "I'll probably need to hire two or three more guys, to help out me and Blake. And I'll need to get materials and all of that. I don't need to be paid for it, but I'll have to pay the others, of course. And we'll have to put a rush on it, since there's no telling when we'll get a big snowfall, or one shapes up to be worse than usual."

Rhonda nodded. "Well, we'll just have to figure it out," she said decisively, and Nora and her father exchanged a look. "We can't very well have an inn without a roof, so we'll sit down and see what can be done to pay for it all. In the meantime, there are cranberry turkey sandwiches for lunch, and homemade kettle chips with that onion dip you like, Aiden, so everyone sit down around the table and we'll have some lunch. I bet you worked up an appetite, up there on the roof."

"Yes, ma'am," Aiden said with a chuckle, retreating to the table with Donovan and Nora. Nora sat down, feeling a weight on her shoulders. The inn was quiet other than the four of them, Margo was upstairs sleeping, and most of the guests were out and about. It should have been a nice family lunch, but she couldn't shake the worries that were plaguing her.

She went out to the living room after lunch, standing by the Christmas tree and looking at the individual decorations, some of which she remembered putting on the tree as children. Rhonda loved seeing the collection of ornaments grow year after year, and some of them had been on the tree for thirty or more Christmases. And then there were some that Rhonda had inherited from her own mother.

Nora heard Aiden walking up behind her, and she turned to look at her husband. She'd thought her emotions were under control, but seeing his handsome, kind, patient face undid her a little, and she felt tears well up, one escaping and dripping down her cheek.

Aiden immediately stepped forward, catching it with his thumb and brushing it away. He enveloped her in a hug, pulling her against his broad chest, and Nora breathed in the familiar scent of him—cedar and maplewood, his spicy aftershave, and the warm scent of her husband. It made her feel a little better, for a moment.

"It's all going to be okay," he said, and Nora sighed against his chest.

"It's all a lot though," she said, looking up at him. "Mom likes to say they'll figure it out, but I did that business plan for them two years ago with Caroline, so I have a pretty good idea of the inn's finances.

They don't have the money to pay for those repairs. And I want to help, but I know we can't right now. My mom worries about Caroline and me getting along with Margo while she's here, and we're both trying, but there's..."

She sighed. "Well, there's a lot of history there, and a lot of stuff we haven't talked about. And now Margo has broken her leg, so she needs help. I normally would help so much more with all of this, but the baby..."

She trailed off, sniffing back tears, and Aiden ran a comforting hand down her back as he kissed the side of her head.

"It's going to be all right," he promised her, standing there in the twinkling lights of the Christmas tree. "I know it sounds trite. But we will figure it out. I'll find a way to get your parents' roof fixed. Margo will settle in. And this will be a good Christmas like it always is."

Nora nodded, leaning against him as she reached up to wipe her eyes. She wasn't sure how everything was going to work out. But he was right about one thing.

With her husband and surrounded by her family, every Christmas was a good one.

CHAPTER EIGHT

The smell of fresh coffee gave Spencer a boost as he walked into The Mellow Mug, and he breathed in, sure he could smell the cinnamon of Melanie's pastries underneath it. The shop was all decked out for the holidays, a tree twinkling in the corner, and he walked up to the register to order his usual: a peppermint white mocha. He drank standard coffee most of the time, with just a little cream, but during the holidays he liked the festive flavor. He'd never had time for drinking a fancy latte before work when he was in San Francisco, and it felt like a reminder of just one of the reasons that he enjoyed being here in Evergreen Hollow.

"Is that all?" Melanie asked as she rang him up, and he hesitated for just a moment.

"I'll get a cinnamon brown sugar latte as well," he said, giving in to the impulse. He had planned to check in on Margo, and he thought it would be a nice gesture. Hopefully, she would appreciate the thought, and maybe he'd get a smile out of her. He thought she was probably feeling down, stuck being off her feet with a broken leg.

Just being neighborly, he told himself as he collected the coffees and headed out to his car, but as he set them down and started the engine, *Jingle Bells* filling the small space as the radio came on, he had to admit that it was also because he wanted to do something special for her. He had liked her from the start, and he wished they'd met in a different capacity. An after-hours visit for a broken leg definitely wasn't the most romantic of settings.

He parked in front of The Mistletoe Inn, grabbing both coffees, and knocked on the door. Rhonda Stoker answered it—he knew her from the times she'd visited his office—and he smiled at her.

"Morning. Can I come in? I wanted to check on Margo. See how that leg is holding up."

A broad smile crossed Rhonda's face at that. "Of course you can." She opened the door wider, stepping back. "Come on in. Margo is in the living room. Is that for her?" She nodded at the cup in his hand, a knowing look on her face.

"It is." He flashed her a smile. "Just a little pick-me-up."

"Margo's always glad for another cup of coffee." Rhonda beamed at him, and then hurried off toward the back of the inn, leaving him alone to head into the living room.

He saw Margo immediately, as soon as he walked in. She was sitting in an armchair next to the fireplace, her leg in its cast propped up on an ottoman, and he could see in an instant that she was restless. Her crutches were propped within reaching distance, a book was flopped open and face down on the table next to her, and she had a video playing on her phone, but it was lying in her lap. It was clear she couldn't focus on anything, and she had a dejected expression on her face that tugged at his heartstrings.

Until she looked up and saw him standing there, and her face brightened instantly.

He knew he shouldn't read too much into that. She was possibly just glad to see anyone, bored out of her mind as she probably was. But he liked seeing her face brighten up like that for him. It made him glad he'd decided to drop by and bring her the coffee.

"I thought I'd come and see you, make sure you

were all right. And bring you some caffeine—not that you have anywhere for the energy to go right now," he joked. The moment he said it, he wondered if it would strike a nerve instead of being funny.

Fortunately, Margo seemed to see the humor in it. She smiled as he handed her the coffee, immediately taking a sip of it. "Oh, that's good," she said. "Nora said the coffee shop in town was something else. I hadn't had a chance to go yet, but it really is good. I guess her best friend owns it."

"Your sister's best friend? I didn't know that." Spencer smiled, nodding at the chair next to Margo. "All right if I sit down?"

"Of course." She took another sip of her latte. "You don't have appointments?"

"Nothing until this afternoon. And the nurses can take care of any walk-ins for a bit. Unless there's another accident on the ski slopes." He winked at her. "How are you doing? Any pain?"

"Oh, so this is an official visit." She was still smiling though. "A little at night. I think when the meds start to wear off, and when I start getting tired around then, it starts to get achy. A little bit of stabbing pain, sometimes. But nothing like when I first broke it."

Spencer leaned forward, looking at the cast.

"This is all holding up well. You're following all the instructions?"

"Yes, doctor." She said it sarcastically, but with a hint of humor, and he thought to himself that he liked the way she said it more than he probably should.

"I thought you were a tourist. But you must have grown up here—I haven't been here long, but I know the history of this place, at least." He looked at her curiously. "Home for the holidays?"

"Something like that." Margo shifted in her seat, and he thought he felt a little uneasiness from her, but he decided not to pry. "What about you? You said you moved here a year ago? Where from?"

She asked her questions with a surprising directness, and he remembered that she'd said she was a journalist. A photojournalist, but that probably still involved some interviewing, he imagined. He didn't mind. "I came from San Francisco," he said easily. "I used to work at one of the big hospitals there, right out of medical school. But when my father needed someone to take over the practice, I decided to leave and move here. It was a big decision, but one I'm glad I made."

"You like being a small-town doctor?" Margo looked at him quizzically, and Spencer nodded.

"I love it," he said sincerely. "The pace is different, and I didn't realize how much I needed that until I was in it. And I feel like I matter to these people. Not that I didn't matter, in San Francisco. I know I was doing important work there too. But it's more personal, here. It's hard to explain, exactly. But I haven't regretted the change a bit. And it gives me some time to myself, which is nice. No mornings like this, working at the hospital in the city."

Margo blinked slowly at him, a small smile on her lips as she took another drink of her latte. "So you're saying you didn't bring every patient who fell victim to unfortunate circumstances a personal cinnamon latte?"

He felt his face flush immediately at that. He couldn't help it, and he knew from the way her smile grew that she'd noticed. She'd been trying to see if she could get a bit of a rise out of him, and she'd succeeded.

"How long will it take for this to get better?" Margo asked, gesturing at her leg. "A few weeks?"

Spencer winced. "Six to twelve," he said honestly. "If you follow all of the instructions, and take good care of it, and don't overdo things, it'll be more toward the lower end of that, hopefully.

Otherwise, you're looking at a solid twelve, if not more."

Margo's face fell instantly. "Oh," she said softly, and he could feel her disappointment. It was palpable.

He could tell she was used to being on the go. She was clearly someone who was typically active and outgoing, and this injury had taken the wind out of her sails. It was undoubtedly marring what would probably have otherwise been a good visit home.

He didn't say anything out loud. But to himself, he resolved to find a way to make it up to her.

He wanted to make her time back in Evergreen Hollow as memorable as it possibly could be.

CHAPTER NINE

Three days in, Margo's broken leg was making her stir crazy. She hadn't left since Nora and Caroline had brought her back from the doctor's office, and even though she knew an outing with her sisters was likely going to be awkward, she was desperate.

So when Caroline arrived that morning and she overheard her and Rhonda discussing Caroline going out for supplies for the inn, she jumped at the chance to go.

"Want someone to tag along?" she asked as Caroline walked back into the living room. "I could use some fresh air."

Caroline gave her a small smile. "Well, I already have a co-pilot. Jay is with me today. But we wouldn't mind some company, if you want to go."

Margo felt a jab of curiosity at that. She hadn't met Caroline's stepson yet. Honestly, it was hard for her to imagine her older sister with kids. Caroline wasn't the most patient person in the world, and as far as she knew, it took a good bit of patience to deal with children. But Caroline seemed happy about the situation, and she was interested to meet her new step-nephew.

"All right. Sounds good to me." She pushed herself awkwardly out of the armchair she was sitting in, wincing as she reached for her crutches. Everything she did felt slow and clumsy and awkward now, and she hated it.

She hobbled down the steps, following Caroline to her car. There was a small boy who looked about eight or nine sitting in the back, his glasses sliding down his nose as he traipsed a pair of plastic dinosaurs back and forth over the back of the passenger's seat.

"Don't bump Aunt Margo," Caroline warned as she slid into the driver's side, after opening the door for Margo. Margo twisted around, offering Jay a smile.

"I don't mind," she said, and she really didn't. In the grand scheme of things, getting bumped by a toy dinosaur in the back of the head wasn't all that bad.

It definitely didn't compare to losing her job or breaking a leg, and that was about where she was these days. "It's nice to meet you, Jay."

"Nice to meet you too!" Jay said brightly, before knocking the Tyrannosaurus Rex and the triceratops together. "Rawr!"

"You'll have to excuse him," Caroline said, a small smile on her face as she pulled out of the driveway and onto the main road. "He really has a thing for dinosaurs, and fossils. We've watched *Jurassic Park* three times this holiday break alone, and it just started. Rhett is picking up the rest of the movies at the secondhand video store today, just so we can introduce him to something different. Maybe even a Godzilla movie, just to spice it up."

She laughed, and Margo felt herself smiling too. This new version of her sister wasn't so bad. It was just odd.

"I heard the most recent one was good," Margo offered, even though she didn't really have any idea. She hadn't been to a movie theater in a long time. She was used to only having a week or so in Jersey between assignments, and those were usually spent late at the office, finishing up articles and then preparing for the next trip. Every once in a while she'd get a ticket just for herself, buy one of those big boxes of Junior Mints and go see something, but it was a rare occasion. She couldn't actually remember what the movie had been the last time she'd done that.

"Mom said you moved into the cabin at the back of the property." She glanced over at Caroline. "Do you like it?"

Caroline nodded. "Rhett and I fixed it up after he asked me to marry him."

Margo snuck a glance at her sister's wedding finger as she spoke. A simple gold band with a floral pattern etched into it—no diamond ring to be seen. It fit what she would have pictured for Caroline.

"Rhett actually bought a house when he first moved to Evergreen Hollow," Caroline continued. "But he understood how much the inn means to me, and how important it is to me to be close to it. Of course, neither of us wanted to live under the same roof with Mom and Dad, that would have been awkward. But the house on the property was a good compromise. Rhett didn't mind. He didn't have a major attachment to the house he bought. We're actually renting it out now."

"Wow," Margo breathed.

For one thing, it was more sentences strung together than she remembered her sister saying the last time she was home. For another, she was really happy that Caroline had found Rhett. She still didn't know him very well—she'd only met him twice since she'd been back home—but it was clear that he understood what mattered to Caroline, and wanted to make her happy. As far as Margo was concerned, she didn't really think anything else mattered.

Caroline turned into the parking lot of the Sugar Maple General Store and turned off the engine.

"We've got to run a quick errand here," she told Jay, glancing in the rearview mirror. "If you're patient, I'll make sure to get a sleeve of that maple candy Leon sells."

"Bribery?" Margo teased, and her sister gave her a narrow look before sliding out of the car.

Margo had never minded the snow before, but on crutches, it was absolutely miserable. She had to be extra careful to make sure she didn't hit any patches of ice, and trying to pick them up and put them back down anywhere that the snow had built up was an exercise in patience she didn't have. But she couldn't exactly regret coming out. The sun was bright, glinting off the neatly plowed white snowdrifts, everything was decorated for Christmas and festive, and the cold air felt bracing after being cooped up inside of the inn.

She sucked in a deep breath as she nudged the car door closed behind her, and followed Caroline and Jay inside.

"Caroline!" Leon called out as they walked in. "And—oh my stars, is that Margo?"

Margo felt herself flush. She hadn't been out and about in town when she first arrived, and after the accident, she'd stayed in until today.

Leon's expression reminded her of why she had avoided a lot of the small-town haunts. He looked genuinely excited to see her, but it all felt a little too prodigal daughter for her taste, and she shifted uncomfortably.

"Margo! It's so good to see you." Leon's wife, Bethany, came out from behind the counter, smelling faintly of spices. Margo awkwardly returned the hug she gave her, breathing in the smell of biscuit dough and thyme.

Some things never change, she thought with amusement.

When Bethany wasn't working next door at her pet grooming salon, she cleaned off the pet hair and made the biscuit sandwiches that the general shop sold at their hot food counter a couple of days a week. Margo vividly remembered the taste of one of those sandwiches after school, back when she was younger.

"Are you home for long?" Bethany asked.

The genuine curiosity in her voice, without any kind of expectation or judgment, set Margo a little more at ease. She didn't usually like the small-town shtick of everyone here, but there was a comforting warmth to Bethany that didn't give her that feeling she so often got with anyone else.

"A little while," Margo said vaguely.

The truth was that she didn't know how long she was going to be staying. She couldn't afford to keep her apartment indefinitely without working, but with her leg broken, she wasn't sure what she was going to do. She couldn't just hang out in Evergreen Hollow, and she wasn't sure that she wanted to. But everything felt up in the air.

"Well, we're glad to have you for as long as you want to be here," Bethany said warmly, and it felt like she genuinely meant it. She'd always had a disarming nature, Margo thought, something to do with the way that it always felt like her focus was all on the person she was talking to, and she really was interested in what they had to say.

"Margo? Are you ready to go?" Caroline was holding two paper bags of supplies, while Jay had a sleeve of candy in his small fist, one hand already sticky.

"Sure. Bye, Bethany." Margo gave her a smile, and Bethany returned it.

"Come back whenever you feel up to it. We're always glad to see you."

Margo started to hobble after Caroline, only to see the door open just before they reached it, and stop dead in her tracks.

She saw jet black hair and a full, well-groomed beard on a tall man in a green flannel shirt, and she knew immediately who it was.

Chris Long, her ex-fiancé, and the last man she wanted to run into while she was home.

She'd just started to feel a little better about being back in Evergreen Hollow, and now all she wanted was to run away again.

"Can we hurry up and get out to the car?" she hissed at Caroline as Chris went to the left.

Caroline shot her an odd look, but nudged Jay ahead of her, the two of them picking up pace as they walked out to Caroline's sedan. Margo yanked open the passenger's door herself, nearly slipping in the snow as she threw herself into the car and yanked down the mirror to try and hide her face, just in case

Chris looked out the window or came out right after them.

She heard the sound of the trunk shutting, and Caroline slid into the car a moment later.

"What on earth was that about?" Caroline asked, looking and sounding completely baffled. "What got into you?"

Margo let out a sharp breath. She didn't like admitting what had bothered her so much, but she knew she couldn't just blow it off. Caroline wasn't just going to let that go.

"Chris came in," she said flatly. "I saw him just as we were leaving. I really didn't want him to see *me*."

Caroline's face softened at that. "You know," she said gently, "I never agreed with how Chris handled that whole situation. It was a real cowardly thing to do."

It was an olive branch, an attempt to be understanding, and Margo saw it for what it was and reached out for it.

"I thought it would have stopped hurting by now," she admitted. "But there's still some of it there, unfortunately. It still stings, seeing him."

"I understand." Caroline looked at her with a hint of sympathy. "But even so, that wasn't a reason to desert your hometown and all the people in it, Margo."

Just like that, she felt all her walls snap back up. *There it is.* Leave it to Caroline to take a moment of connection and turn it into a lecture, she thought, leaning back against the seat and facing forward again. "I left for other reasons," she said sharply. "I have a job to do, you know."

Had a job to do. Her sister didn't say it, but she didn't need to. Margo was already thinking it, the words echoing in her head as she looked out of the window. The conversation had gone right back where she'd expected it to.

But, in spite of that, it had felt good to feel a moment's understanding from her sister. To connect with her, just for a second.

It made her feel ever so slightly hopeful that maybe it would happen again.

CHAPTER TEN

That evening, the inn was full—not just with guests, but with all of the Stokers and their in-laws. Nora and Aiden, Caroline, Jay and Rhett, Margo, and Rhonda and Donovan were all sitting in the living room around the roaring fire, a platter of Rhonda's homemade gingerbread cookies and mulled apple ciders in front of them.

It had the feeling of a cheery evening, but it was weighed down by the news about the roof. Margo had been filled in on the situation, and she felt the same sense of despair that everyone else seemed to. She hadn't been home in a long time, but she knew enough to know that the inn wasn't rolling in money, and a whole new roof was no cheap endeavor. It made her feel even more guilty about the fact that she'd come home at least partially because it was a place to stay that would make stretching her meagre savings easier.

"I talked to a couple of guys from the next town over," Aiden said, reaching for a cookie. "I can definitely get some help. And they're willing to do it in the time frame we need without charging rush prices. But getting the materials here fast will be an issue, so there's that. I've got some of what I need, but Leon is going to have to put in an order for me, and soon."

"I looked over the books today," Caroline said, glancing over at Rhonda. "If we delay replacing the radiators that need it in any rooms that aren't guest rooms, we might be able to manage it. But even so, it's going to be tight."

"We can't run an inn without a roof." Rhonda raised her hands and let them fall back into her lap. "And there isn't any good time of year for this to happen. Summer, maybe, would have been best. But if it's not snowing, there's the chance of rain. We just have to figure it out."

"There's got to be some way to get the inn what it needs," Nora said, biting her lip. "We always figure things out, you're right, Mom. We can do it again. We just need to think."

"I'm thinking about some more cider," Rhonda said decisively. "Honey, can you help me?" She looked at Donovan, and the sisters knew the question was about more than just cider—their mother wanted a moment alone to talk this over with their father.

Margo looked around the group, feeling, as usual, a little like the odd one out. Everyone was a family now. Their parents, of course, the same rock-steady couple that they'd been for their children's whole lives, a model of a good relationship and parents Margo was grateful to have, even if she'd put so much distance between herself and her home.

But now her sisters were all coupled up and settled down too, and it was so glaringly obvious in a setting like this. Nora and Aiden were sitting next to each other on the couch, embarrassingly loved-up for a couple that weren't newlyweds any longer, and Nora's baby bump was adorably visible under her red Christmas sweater.

Caroline and Rhett were sitting in wing chairs next to each other, Jay playing on the floor between them with his dinosaurs, and it was more domestic than anything Margo had ever pictured for her sister.

But Caroline looked happy. They all looked happy. And she sat there, wondering how it was that she'd had some of the biggest dreams of any of them, only to come back home feeling like she'd hit a dead end.

Slammed into it hard enough to actually break her leg. She glared down at the cast. It was really insult to injury in every possible way.

"Did you catch the hockey game?" Rhett leaned over to talk to Aiden, who turned toward his brother-in-law, eager to turn to a lighter topic. Caroline moved so that she was closer to Nora and Margo, and Nora drummed her fingers against her chin, clearly deep in thought.

"They can't just drain every last cent," Nora murmured to Caroline. "This house is so old. There's always something going wrong, you know that better than anyone. It'll always be catch-up after this. Even the smallest repairs will start feeling monumental because there won't be enough to cover them."

"Dad said something about a mortgage for equity." Caroline bit her lip. "I hate it. This place is theirs free and clear. And even if the payments shouldn't be any big deal—which they wouldn't be— it's just the principle of it. And what if something happens? Another slow season? I just can't get behind it. And I know he doesn't either. He's just not sure what to do."

"Of course he doesn't want to do that." Nora shook her head. "This inn is going to go to you eventually, we all know that. It would essentially be mortgaging your family's future. We can't let him feel like he needs to do that."

"No. But what else is there?" Caroline blew out a sharp breath. "Neither of us have the extra, or we would have already offered."

Nora pressed her fingers to her temples, letting out a slow breath. "I don't know what to do," she admitted. "I don't have any solutions."

"What about a fundraiser?" Margo spoke up before she could talk herself out of it, leaning forward a little in her seat. "Everyone is always saying that the people who live in Evergreen Hollow are all about helping each other. And the inn has been here forever. Why not try to raise the money to fix it?"

Nora looked around at Margo, startled. "You think people would donate money to the roof repair?"

Margo shrugged. "Mistletoe Inn is special to Evergreen Hollow, right? Everyone looks forward to Mom's Christmas decorations every year. It's the only place for tourists to stay, which also means that it supports all the other businesses that depend on the tourism. It's a part of this place. I would think people would want to help because of that."

Nora and Caroline glanced at each other. There was a flicker of doubt there, but Caroline finally raised her eyebrows, settling back in her chair.

"You might be on to something," she said, and Nora nodded.

"I don't know if it would work, but it might be at least worth trying. Aiden said time was of the essence for the roof, so we'd need to put together something pretty quickly."

"A Christmas bake-off?" Margo suggested. "Or maybe something with the festival."

"The festival is too far away." Caroline shook her head. "By that time, the problem with the roof will probably have gotten a lot worse. We need something that can help sooner."

"What about a Christmas tree decorating contest?" Nora looked at the other two women, glancing over and dropping her voice as she saw Rhonda and Donovan walking back into the room. "Everyone loves a friendly competition, and it's perfect for this time of year."

"That sounds like it could go over really well." Margo looked over at Caroline, who nodded.

"Let's see what we can come up with and give it

a try," Caroline agreed, and Margo felt a sudden, surprising swell of happiness.

She hadn't really wanted to get involved with anything that had to do with Evergreen Hollow. Her plan had been to only come home long enough to get her head straight after the layoff, and then move on to the next thing. But this wasn't really about Evergreen Hollow, it was about her family. And after so long away, it felt nice to have them be excited about something that she'd had a hand in.

It wouldn't fix everything, but maybe it would repair things a little.

CHAPTER ELEVEN

The next day, Margo convinced Caroline to drop her off at Rockridge Grill for lunch, while Caroline ran errands. The food was fantastic—she'd had a few spots back in Jersey that she really liked, but nothing could quite compare to how good the food she'd had since coming back was. She'd always known her mother was an exceptional cook, of course, but she was surprised at how good this was.

She'd ordered a tuna melt and fries and had been delivered a sandwich twice the size of what she'd expected, with fresh-made tuna salad on sourdough, and melty local cheddar cheese on top. The fries were thin and crispy, just how she liked them, and they came with a lemon garlic aioli that went perfectly with the fish.

She nibbled at it while she looked over the notepad she'd brought with her, that had a list of ideas she and her sisters had gathered for the fundraiser.

Build-a-Tree, the name they'd given the Christmas-tree-decorating contest, was scrawled at the top of the page, with a list of jotted-down notes under it that they'd put together the night before.

Margo was still surprised that they'd liked her idea so much. She hadn't expected them to take her seriously—in fact, she'd really expected the exact opposite when she'd suggested it. For them to brush her off, to say she couldn't possibly know what would work, when she'd been gone for so long.

But instead, she was looking at the fruit of that suggestion on the list in front of her, and this was something that the three of them were doing together. She couldn't remember the last time that had happened.

She was just underlining a note about concessions for the contest when she saw someone approaching her table out of the corner of her eye. She looked up abruptly, and her heart did a somersault in her chest when she saw that it was Spencer standing there.

He really was too handsome for his own good—

and hers, she thought. She didn't think she'd ever had such a handsome doctor before. And here he was, out of the office, standing there smiling at her, clearly taking time out of his day to come and intentionally say hi.

She managed a smile herself, feeling a flutter of nervousness as she looked at him. "Did you come over to tell me that I'm not abiding by doctor's orders by being out and about?"

Spencer chuckled. "Oh, I don't know about that. I think fresh air and socializing with others is great medicine. I think you're abiding by my prescribed recovery plan just fine," he said teasingly. "As long as you're not planning on driving yourself home," he added quickly.

"Oh, no," Margo assured him. "Definitely not. Caroline is going to come pick me up."

"Well then." Spencer smiled. "Nothing to worry about."

She knew there was no real purpose in inviting him to sit down and chat for a minute. The broken leg might have trapped her in Evergreen Hollow for a bit longer than she'd planned, but she had no intentions of staying any longer than she strictly needed to. As soon as she recovered, she still planned on leaving.

But he was standing there looking at her, with his easy, amiable air and handsome face, a body altogether nicer than what she thought any doctor needed to have, his blond hair and sparkling hazel eyes—and she couldn't resist the urge to get to know him a little better. She didn't want him to walk away just yet, and she gave in to the urge, even though she knew it wasn't going to go anywhere.

"Do you want to sit down?" she invited. "If you don't have anywhere else you need to be just yet."

"Sure." Spencer flashed her another of those wide smiles. "I'm not in any hurry. Long lunches are definitely one of the perks of this small-town doctor life."

Margo laughed at that, as he slid into the opposite side of the booth. "I used to eat lunch at my desk when I was in the office," she admitted. "But I didn't spend a lot of time there. I was always traveling. A lot of lunches on the go."

"You said you're a photojournalist, right?" He looked at her with a keen interest in his eyes. "That seems like an exciting job."

"It is. *Was*," she corrected herself, with a fresh pang of hurt in her chest. "I was laid off."

Spencer made a sympathetic sound, clicking his tongue against his teeth. "I'm sorry to hear that," he said, and Margo thought he sounded sincere. "It's a bad time of year for that to happen."

Margo nodded. "I came back home to—I don't know. Think about things, I guess. It seemed like the right place to retreat to, at the time. But I haven't been home in years. I avoided coming back here at all, really. So it's been challenging in more ways than one. And now I've found myself wondering if maybe stacking the stress of coming back home after so long on top of a layoff wasn't really the right choice."

"Why did you leave in the first place?" Spencer asked curiously. "If you don't mind my asking, that is."

"No, I don't mind." She let out a slow breath, remembering as she did that she'd had a tuna sandwich for lunch, and she fought the urge to touch her hand to her mouth with embarrassment. But Spencer didn't seem to notice anything, and she couldn't bring herself to care all that much. He had the most beautiful eyes she thought she'd ever seen on a man, hazel with just the right amount of green, and he was looking at her as if he was genuinely interested in everything she might have to say. So she kept talking.

"I was engaged to a guy right out of high school. Local guy. Planned to stick around, marry him, the whole small-town nine yards. And then he went to go help out his grandparents that first summer after we graduated, and he met someone else. He didn't tell me about it either. He made all kinds of excuses for it later, when I found out, but at the end of the day..."

She shrugged, pressing her lips thinly together. "He still did what he did. We couldn't fix things, and I don't know that he really wanted to. I'd always wanted to see the world. I'd been willing to stick around for him because I was young and thought he was the love of my life and all that, but afterward, I just wanted to get as far away from Evergreen Hollow and all those memories as I could. So I did. I made a job out of going as far away as I could, as often as I could. And now I'm right back here where I started."

There was more bitterness in her voice, at the end, than she'd meant for there to be. But Spencer didn't look judgmental as he looked at her across the table.

"I can understand that," Spencer said slowly. "That's a difficult thing to deal with. And right out of high school too, when you don't even really know what you want your life to be yet. None of that could have been easy." He looked at her with what she thought might be sympathy, or encouragement, or maybe a little of both. "But sometimes you need to give people and places another chance. So maybe that's what you're getting to do right now."

Margo nodded, then pushed the notepad toward him so he could see the list of ideas. "I'm hoping that this fundraiser might be an olive branch with my family. Me helping out with all of this. I haven't handled distance from my hometown all that well, I know that. So maybe this will make a difference."

"There's always time," Spencer told her firmly. "I believe that. You've got time now."

"Doctor Thorpe?" The woman at the takeout counter called out his name, and he gave Margo an apologetic look.

"That's my order. I'd sit and eat with you so we could finish talking, but a couple of the nurses back at the clinic asked me to pick up some lunch for them too, so I've got to get back."

"Of course," Margo agreed quickly, shoving down any disappointment she felt. "It was nice to sit and chat."

"It was." Spencer paused as he stood. "Do you need any help with the fundraiser?"

She felt that somersault in her chest again. Once again too, she had the thought that it was pointless to pursue this. She was going to take off again as soon as the opportunity presented itself, and Spencer clearly had put down firm roots here. But she *did* need help. Nora and Caroline had pointed out over and over what a short time frame they were on to get this done, in order for it to actually help the situation with the roof.

"Sure," she said with a smile. "That would be great."

"Here you go, then." Spencer fished out a business card from his pocket, handing it to her. "Give me a call and let me know what I can help with."

She felt herself blush, just a little. "Okay." She took the card, slipping it into her pocket. "I'll do that."

Margo watched him walk away, going to pick up his food, and she questioned the wisdom of calling him. Of getting herself involved in anything that might give her more of a reason than just her family to miss Evergreen Hollow when she left.

Because she *was* going to leave.

Anything else was just a temporary distraction until then.

CHAPTER TWELVE

Nora thought, not for the first time as she walked into Caroline's house, that it very much suited her sister. It had a cozy, rustic feeling that echoed the inn up the hill, a log cottage with a wraparound porch and three bedrooms, a large living room and a kitchen. It was very domestic, she thought as she slipped her coat off and hung it up on the hook next to the door. She could see toys in the living room by the fireplace, some of Jay's dinos marching across the brick. A scattering of shoes were in the entryway: Caroline's duck boots, a pair of heavier boots that looked like Rhett's, Jay's sneakers, and slippers that could have been either of the adults'.

It smelled like pine from the Christmas tree twinkling in the living room, and Nora walked in to see Margo and Caroline already sitting on the couch looking over a list of details for the fundraiser, a fire crackling merrily in the fireplace just beyond them. There were mugs of hot cocoa sitting on the coffee table, and Margo had her broken leg propped up on an ottoman. It was a warm, cozy scene that gave her hope that maybe things would start to look up, that it wouldn't continue to be so tense among the three of them. That maybe Margo was settling in better, and everything else would be too.

She was actually enjoying being with both of her sisters, at the same time, for the first time in years. And she was beginning to dare to hope that having a project to work on together would make things easier. Something for them to collaborate on, to cut through everything that had piled up over the years. They could keep working on that, she thought as she went to the kitchen to get her own cup of cocoa and then joined them on the sofa, once they'd gotten comfortable with each other again. Just like she had when she'd come back home.

"How is the planning going?" Nora asked as she sank back onto the couch. "Making a list of things we might need?"

Caroline nodded. "And some ancillary ideas for the day of the contest itself. Just brainstorming at this point, still, but I think some of it is beginning to be more concrete." She let out a long breath. "I've been so busy today, between the inn and Jay, that I hadn't really had time to sit down and work on anything for this until right now."

"Where is Jay anyway?" Margo asked, twisting around as if she would see him materialize.

Caroline grimaced. "He's in his room. He didn't do his homework, and Rhett and I have recently set some ground rules about that, so..." She lifted one shoulder in a helpless shrug. "He got his PlayStation temporarily taken away. And he's pretty upset about that, so he went to his room and won't talk to me."

Nora winced, imagining that sort of thing in her own future. "Kids are going to be kids," she said, and Margo laughed at that.

"Remember the time that we swapped out all the Christmas lights for Halloween ones, and Mom got so upset?"

"Oh my goodness," Nora groaned. "I do remember that. There was that time we swapped out the salt for sugar in the dining room before the guests came down for breakfast. We were grounded for a full week after that stunt."

"Caroline never got into trouble though." Margo wrinkled her nose at her older sister. "I think the only time you ever got grounded was that time you forgot to close the gate for the goat pen, and they all got out and Dad had to chase them around in the dark."

"Look, it's not my fault I knew how to follow the rules, and you two were little hellions," Caroline said primly. "And anyway, now I'm getting my comeuppance, right? I have a ten-year-old stepson who is putting new grays in my hair every day." Her face softened as she said it though, and Margo laughed.

"It seems like you love every second," she said, and Caroline shot her a grateful look.

"I'm glad it shows," she said quietly. Then she cleared her throat, sitting up a little straighter as she nudged the notepad in Nora's direction. "Not to get off track—we need volunteers. This thing isn't going to be run by the three of us alone, obviously, we'll need some help."

"Spencer offered to help with whatever he could," Margo ventured, and immediately both of her sisters turned sharply to look at her, confusion on both of their faces.

"Spencer?" Nora asked quizzically, and she didn't fail to notice the way Margo's cheeks pinkened at the question.

"Doctor Thorpe," Margo clarified, and Nora's eyebrows rose.

"You're calling him by his first name now?" Caroline asked, and Margo's blush deepened.

"I've just seen him a few times since the accident, and we've talked, so—I don't know, *Doctor Thorpe* just sounds so unnecessarily formal." She shrugged. "It's not a big deal."

"Mm-hm." Nora wasn't about to let it go so easily. "Mom said he brought you coffee the other day, right after your accident. I can't say I recall hearing from anyone else in town that *Spencer* has been bringing them lattes and making in-house calls," she teased, and Margo narrowed her eyes.

"That's true," Caroline said thoughtfully, an unusual glimmer of mischief in her own eyes. "I do remember Mom telling me about that. And didn't you mention that you saw him at lunch the other day?" A smile lifted the corner of one side of her mouth. "Is that when he volunteered to help?"

"Is it?" Nora's eyes were bright with curiosity. "Come on, Margo," she added when she saw the stubborn look on Margo's face that she knew so well. "I want to know about this new relationship with the handsome town doctor! You're holding out on us."

"I'm *not*," Margo insisted. "It's not a *relationship.*

We've talked a little, and yes, I think he's good-looking, but..." She trailed off as Nora and Caroline exchanged a look. "Oh my gosh. There's nothing going on. There's nothing that's *going* to go on."

"Does he know that?" Nora teased playfully. "Because the personally delivered lattes imply that he's not aware of all of this *nothing* that's going on."

Margo shot her a deadly glare, but Nora didn't mind a bit. In fact, if anything, the conversation warmed her down to her toes.

It felt like old times, but a little different now, now that they were all grown up. She remembered clearly the three of them crowded on a bed as teenagers, talking about crushes and giggling over boys. The sense of nostalgia tugged at her heart, and looking at her two sisters, she felt a renewed hope that everything was going to be all right.

That this year, the Christmas miracle would be Margo's.

CHAPTER THIRTEEN

Once again, Spencer found himself standing in The Mellow Mug in the mid-morning, trying to decide whether or not he should pick something up for Margo as well.

This time, instead of a doctor-patient visit, he was going to a business meeting at The Mistletoe Inn. Margo, Nora, Caroline, and Rhonda were sitting down to discuss the fundraiser, and Margo had called him the day before, telling him they would love to take him up on his offer of help and asking if he would like to join them. He'd said yes, of course, because he had genuinely wanted to help— and now he was staring at a glass case of pastries, wondering if bringing an extra along sent the wrong message, or the right one.

"Something on your mind?" Melanie teased as she walked up to the counter, eyeing where he was staring intently at the options. "You're having the hardest time picking a pastry that I think I've ever seen anyone have."

"I guess I am, aren't I?" he asked ruefully, a smile quirking the corner of his mouth, and Melanie laughed.

"Well, what do you normally like?"

"It's not for me. I was thinking of bringing Margo one," he said, the admission coming out before he had a chance to think better of it. He thought that maybe he should have kept that to himself the moment he saw Melanie's eyes light up at that information.

"Oh. Well, in that case..." Melanie bit her lip, grinning. "I happen to know she *loves* cinnamon. And maple. So these would be perfect." She pointed at a tray of cinnamon rolls coated in a thick layer of creamy maple frosting. "But she's also partial to peppermint. So the peppermint chocolate croissants would be a good choice as well."

"I'll take two of the maple cinnamon rolls, then," Spencer said. "Along with my caramel macchiato."

"I was so happy to hear that Margo finally came back home to visit," Melanie said as she rang up his purchase, glancing up at him and sliding the container of cinnamon rolls over. "I keep hoping that maybe she'll find a reason to stay in town. We were good friends in school, you know. I'd love for her to move back for good."

She didn't say outright that she thought *he* might be the reason for Margo to stay, but the insinuation was there. It was there in the mischievous glint in her eyes as she handed him the pastries and the smile on her face as she gave him his coffee, and Spencer found himself momentarily wondering if he was being a bit too transparent when it came to his interest in Margo. It seemed like people were able to see right through him, and he thought maybe that meant Margo could too. If she could, she hadn't done anything about it yet.

That feeling was only compounded when he arrived at the inn. He knocked on the door and Rhonda let him in, the same knowing look on her face that Melanie had had, as if everyone were sharing an inside joke about him and he was only partially in on it. It made him feel slightly off-kilter, and he wasn't sure how he felt about that.

"Margo's in the living room," Rhonda said as if that were the only piece of information that mattered, and then she led the way, letting him follow as they walked into the warm, pine-and-cinnamon-scented space. A fire was crackling, the Christmas tree twinkling, and it was full of a sense of holiday coziness that he was fairly sure was impossible to get anywhere else. The Mistletoe Inn was the center point of everything Christmas in the town, he thought, and he could see why it meant so much to everyone. Why Margo and her sisters had come up with this idea, feeling sure that the community would help.

Margo was sitting in the living room, her leg propped up on an ottoman in its cast. She had a notebook open on her lap, a mug of coffee in front of her, and he was pleased to see a smile wreathe her face when she looked up and saw him.

He was just about to tell Margo he'd brought her breakfast when Nora walked into the room. The minute she caught sight of him, he was absolutely certain that he saw that same knowing look on her face that he'd seen on Melanie and Rhonda.

Nora crossed the room to her mother, linking their arms together as she tugged Rhonda toward the kitchen. "We should leave them alone," she said in a voice pitched low enough that it sounded as if it were meant to not be heard, but Spencer knew she'd actually meant for him at least to overhear, if not

Margo too. It would have been comical if he weren't so unsure how to handle it all. It was starting to feel as if the whole town was plotting something.

"Do you want a breakfast burrito, Spencer?" Rhonda asked. "I made them fresh this morning."

One of the pastries in the box was supposed to be his, but he didn't think he could turn down the allure of Rhonda's cooking. "That sounds great," he said. "Thank you."

"We'll go get it, then," Nora chimed in, once again tugging her mother toward the kitchen, and in a matter of minutes Spencer was alone with Margo in the living room.

He gave her a lopsided smile. "I brought you a cinnamon roll," he said, setting the box down on the table in front of her. "Fresh from The Mellow Mug. Melanie recommended the maple-frosted."

Margo's eyes lit up at that. "So coffee *and* bespoke pastry delivery is something you do for all your patients, then?"

There was a lightly teasing note to her voice that gave him hope. Surely she was seeing the same thing he was, how everyone was behaving around them, but she hadn't completely clammed up and closed off, and that made him think there might be some possibility that she shared his interest. He sat down next to her with his own cup of coffee, glancing at the notebook in her lap. "Are these the plans for the contest?"

Margo nodded, picking up a fork and taking a bite of the cinnamon roll. "This is *so* good." She offered him the fork. "I know my mom is bringing you a burrito, but you should try it."

Spencer obligingly took a bite. It *was* delicious, he'd had Melanie's cinnamon rolls before, but they were always delightfully amazing. Soft and doughy, full of spice mixed with the thick maple sweetness, and always a treat.

"We'll have you there as first aid," Margo said, turning the notebook so that he could see the lists she'd made. "Just in case of any injuries, any mishaps. Someone breaking an ornament and cutting a finger or something like that."

She laughed at the silliness of the idea, but Spencer wasn't so sure it was completely out of the question. He'd been a doctor long enough to know that accidents could happen anytime, even when you least expected them.

"Outside of that, if you could help us get our hands on some tents that we could use, that would be amazing," she continued "We're going to have different stations for everyone participating. Hot apple cider, Christmas cookies, that kind of thing. So we could use some tents for the setup."

As she was saying it, Rhonda walked in with a breakfast burrito cut in half on a plate, and she set it down in front of Spencer.

"Enjoy!" she said brightly, just before turning around and heading back into the kitchen where Nora hadn't yet emerged.

The burrito looked delicious. From what Spencer could see, it looked like sausage and cheese, both of which were likely local, along with tomato, avocado, and some kind of sauce. He couldn't help but feel like Rhonda delivering it neatly cut down the middle was a hint that he wasn't supposed to miss.

"We should probably talk about the elephant in the room," Margo said with a small laugh, as if she'd heard what he was thinking. "My family seems to think we're 'getting to know each other.'"

She said it in quotes, smirking a little, and he felt a small weight in his chest. She seemed to think the idea was ridiculous, and he was coming to terms with the fact that he didn't think it was such a ludicrous idea.

"I can see how they got that idea too," she mused with that same small smile on her lips. "Seeing as how you've been going so far above and beyond the normal care of a doctor for his patient. You do seem to be especially invested in my recovery."

Spencer couldn't help smiling at that. "I wouldn't mind 'getting to know you,'" he said, putting the same teasing emphasis on the words that she had. "Depending on how you feel about it."

Margo's teasing smirk faltered a little. "I'm going to be leaving once my leg heals," she pointed out. "My stay got extended a little, but it doesn't change anything. I'll be going back to Jersey once I figure things out—or maybe somewhere else, if I get a job soon enough."

Again, he felt that small drop, a sense of disappointment that she already had one foot out of the door. But he didn't see any reason to close off all possibilities, just because she'd made up her mind about that. He'd spent his life being open to possibility, and this seemed like just one more that was worth pursuing, and seeing where it went.

"We could just enjoy each other's company while you *are* here," he suggested. "What's the harm in that? I think we get along pretty well." He smiled at her, and to his surprise and pleasure, she smiled back.

Even more surprising was her response a

moment later, as she took another bite of the cinnamon roll he'd brought for her.

"You're right," she said, picking up her coffee and wrapping her hands around it. "There's not any harm in just enjoying each other's company. As long as that's all it is."

It felt like a very small victory, one that he was happy to have gotten. And in that moment, he was happy to just be sitting there with her, enjoying her company as she talked about the festival.

The fact that she was enjoying it too only made him that much happier.

CHAPTER FOURTEEN

On Sunday afternoon, Margo and Caroline went into town to make the rounds and discuss details with everyone who had volunteered to help with the event. Caroline had suggested that maybe it would be better if she stayed home since she was still on crutches, but Margo had stubbornly assured her that she could handle it.

Evergreen Hollow was good about keeping the sidewalks and pathways clear of snow and ice, and she'd have felt even more stir crazy if she stayed in the inn for too long. She was used to being on the go, traveling from place to place, researching people and locations and wandering towns in search of the perfect shots, and now she was limited to only as far as she could go before she started getting exhausted on her crutches.

It made her feel a little like she was losing her mind. She didn't want to be grateful for a leaky roof at the inn, knowing what a stressor it was on her parents, but she also couldn't help but think that it had been a *little* bit of a blessing in disguise.

The project to get donations to fix the roof was beginning to bring her and her sisters closer together after all these years of being estranged, and that and her budding friendship with Spencer was really all that was keeping her sane. She felt confident that the roof would be fixed, after all, which made her feel less guilty about being glad that they had this project to work on.

It was impossible *not* to feel confident about it. She'd been right in thinking that everyone in town would want to help contribute, once they found out about the troubles at The Mistletoe Inn, especially since Margo and her sisters had made a holiday mini-festival out of it. A Christmas tree decorating contest was right up the alley of the things Evergreen Hollow residents loved, and the three sisters had definitely struck gold with that plan.

Everyone had something to chip in. Sabrina was running a full-page spread about it in the *Gazette* to build excitement, and the winner would get their picture in the paper along with a slice-of-life interview.

Leon was offering bags of his maple candy as runner-up prizes, as well as offering to run a pancake station for the morning portion of the contest. Bethany had donated a gift certificate to the pet salon as a prize, as well as offering to run the apple cider and hot cocoa stations. Jonathan was overseeing the rest of the food, catered from Rockridge Grill, and both he and the owner of Marie's were donating gift certificates for prizes.

Aidan had already promised to help with bringing in the trees, and Melanie was offering specially designed mugs from The Mellow Mug as part of the prize pool, as well as free coffee through the New Year for the winner.

The best part about all of it, Margo couldn't help but think, is that most of the ideas of what to contribute hadn't been hers or her sisters. They'd come up with the starting points, but everyone had been so eager to chip in that most of them had offered prizes and donations up front.

Her memories of Evergreen Hollow had been mostly bad for a long time, but she was beginning to realize that she'd forgotten about this part of it—how much everyone genuinely wanted to help each other. How happy they all were to chip in and support one another, without expecting anything back. They all knew that if some misfortune were to happen to them, their neighbors would have their backs in turn.

After they left Marie's, the gift certificates for the first, second, and third place winners collected, Margo let out a breath, balancing on her crutches for a moment. "I think I need a break," she admitted. "We've been running around like crazy all morning, and I need to rest for a minute. Can we go sit down somewhere?"

"I could use some coffee," Caroline said. "We'll go to The Mellow Mug and ask Melanie about those coffee cups, and get some caffeine."

"Sounds good to me."

They drove back to The Mellow Mug, and Caroline held the door for her so that she could hobble inside. She gave Caroline her coffee order, a cinnamon dolce latte with extra caramel mixed in, and sank into one of the comfortable armchairs near the back of the cafe.

Her leg was starting to ache, and she had a feeling she knew what Spencer would say if he found out she'd been hopping all over town with Caroline this morning. But honestly, she didn't mind the idea of him sternly chewing her out a little. It meant he cared, which felt nice. It felt good to feel like she mattered to someone outside of her family.

She'd loved her job, but it had meant that friendships were hard to maintain and relationships were usually surface-level at best. It was hard to have anything grow or deepen when she was gone so much of the year. Friendships made in different countries were hard to keep up once she left. Flings overseas were just that. And she'd loved all of it, always felt excited and thrilled by the impermanence of her life—but this was nice too, she found.

She knew she could count on Spencer to care. And even though this was impermanent too, and she'd be moving on once she could, it felt a little more solid than anything she'd had before. *He* felt more solid, more dependable.

Maybe just because he's a doctor, she thought, laughing to herself as she watched Caroline order their coffee and a snack for each of them. Caroline had gotten a piece of spinach quiche for herself, Margo saw, and an apple fritter for her.

Caroline came and sat down a moment later, pushing the fritter and steaming mug of coffee toward Margo, who picked it up and inhaled the smell of cinnamon and caramel. She loved coffee, and she couldn't deny that Melanie made some of the best lattes she'd ever had. A lot of what she'd had in Evergreen Hollow was extra good, she thought. Maybe because it was all made with genuine care and passion, instead of out of sheer necessity or with corporate profits in mind.

"It's nice to have you back," Caroline said after a moment, startling Margo.

Her sister didn't say things like that often. In fact, she was pretty sure Caroline had been the most emotionally open she'd ever known her to be since Margo had been back, and she thought she probably had Nora's return earlier to thank for that. That, and Caroline finding Rhett.

"Has it been nice for you to see everyone again?" Caroline asked after a brief pause.

"It has," Margo admitted. "I have a whole other life though," she reminded Caroline gently, even as she wondered why she felt the need to make sure she constantly followed everything up with that caveat.

She was just afraid, she guessed, that everyone would assume she was going to stay in Evergreen Hollow. That she would follow in Nora's footsteps and reunite the whole Stoker family, and they'd all be settled down in Evergreen Hollow again. She'd only planned on staying for a few days for just that reason because she hadn't wanted anyone to get any ideas. And now, she very much felt the need to make sure that everyone knew she was staying on because of the accident, not because she'd changed her mind.

"I know," Caroline said slowly. "But you don't have that job anymore. I know that must have been really hard. I always knew how much you loved it."

"I always just thought you were mad I left," Margo muttered into her coffee. "I didn't think you really knew anything about what I did, honestly."

"Mom kept up with the magazine you worked for. We read your articles and saw the photos." Caroline paused. "I was upset about you and Nora leaving, yes. You already know, just like Nora does, that I felt as if a lot of the responsibility for our family was pushed onto me, just because I was the only one who stayed. But I've reconciled that feeling."

"I didn't know you read my stuff."

Margo felt her cheeks heat a little, but deep down, she also felt a spark of happiness. She was embarrassed to have assumed that they just didn't care at all, but she was glad that they had. It meant a lot to her that her mother and Caroline had kept up with her, and she wished she'd done a better job of keeping up with them.

"We missed you," Caroline said softly. "And I know you still have one foot in that other life you keep mentioning, and that's okay. But it's also possible that something new is about to begin." She took a slow breath, continuing before Margo could cut in. "It's okay not to be sure about what's going to happen in the future, you know. I still wonder about it all the time."

Margo looked at her curiously. "What do you mean?"

"Ah, well..." Caroline glanced out of the window, taking a sip of her coffee. "Sometimes I don't feel that I'm doing a good job with Jay," she admitted, looking back at Margo. "It's hard to know where to draw the line between being too strict, and too permissive. Rhett falls on the side of the latter a lot, I think. But I don't want to be the evil stepmother who is always laying down the law."

She gave Margo a lopsided smile. "I used to think I was never going to be a mother. After a certain point, I just assumed that time had passed for me. And now here I am." Her smile drooped a little. "I just really have no idea what I'm doing, to be honest. I'm making it up as I go. And a lot of the time I don't think I'm doing it right."

"I think that's just how it is when you have kids,"

Margo said with a laugh. "I don't know either, of course. But that's what I've always heard. And you're doing great," she added encouragingly. "You have a husband and a stepson who love you dearly. And they think you're perfect, which is all that matters."

Margo saw Caroline's face soften as she said it, and she could tell that she'd made her sister feel a little bit better. She was glad of that. But at the same time, it highlighted a little more how empty that other life that she was clinging to, now was.

She'd had her job. That had been her everything, and now it was gone. There was no boyfriend waiting for her, no family, nothing like that even glimmering on the horizon. No gaggle of friends waiting eagerly for her to straighten herself out and return.

There was an empty apartment, and no answers to the handful of papers and magazines that she'd sent her resume out to. That was it. She couldn't help but wonder if maybe Caroline had a point.

That didn't mean she needed to stay in Evergreen Hollow. But maybe being open to something new wasn't such a bad idea.

Maybe she did need to broaden those horizons a little bit.

CHAPTER FIFTEEN

Nora stood over the stove, stirring the pot of beef stew that she was making for dinner, and pressed her hand against her baby bump. Her mind had been full all day, and it wasn't showing any signs of slowing down.

Caroline had called her that morning, asking if she wanted to join her and Margo to go and check in with the businesses in town about their contributions to the tree decorating contest, but she just hadn't felt up to it. She was having a difficult day, and sometimes being around family helped that, but today she just wanted to mull things over without feeling like she was bringing everyone else down.

She felt conflicted and emotional, more so than usual. She'd had bouts of it off and on since getting pregnant, feeling moody and full of worries, but usually, she was able to shake it off pretty easily. Today had been harder than usual.

Margo coming home had definitely added to the emotional weight. She'd missed her sister for so long, just like they all had, and she'd understood the need to get out of Evergreen Hollow.

But Margo had taken it to an extreme, and now she'd just bounced back into their lives. She could see Margo trying to make an effort, with things like her suggestion for how to come up with the funds to fix the inn's roof, but she also knew Margo had every intention of flitting back out of town the moment both of her feet were fine again. She'd always been the more sympathetic one toward it in the past—but she guessed maybe being on the verge of having a daughter of her own was making her look at things differently.

It wasn't that she wasn't grateful. She was glad that Margo had finally come home, even if she felt bad for the circumstances, and she was glad to have had bonding time with both of her sisters. It meant a lot, after so long. And she was beyond stunned and grateful at how much support the community had shown for the fundraiser. It was exactly the example of all the best parts of Evergreen Hollow that had made her want to stay here, beyond being near her family again, and Aiden.

But the fears about becoming a mother kept welling up, and it was harder to quell them lately. It often felt that as soon as she managed to tamp one down, something else would spring up. As soon as she managed to convince herself that she was capable of taking care of a newborn, that the nurses wouldn't be absolutely crazy to send her home with something that fragile and dependent on her, she started worrying about the future.

She was lucky that here, she didn't have all the same worries that she might have had about her daughter going to a public school somewhere like Boston. Rhett had echoed those same thoughts from time to time, about why he'd decided to uproot himself and Jay from Cleveland and come to Evergreen Hollow.

But she still found things to be nervous about. Her daughter getting hurt on the school playground, for instance. Bullied. How to handle social media, which had once been her whole life, and she now cringed at thinking what it would be like when her daughter was old enough to be on the Internet. And with Margo coming home, a new fear had cropped up.

She'd been in Margo's corner all those years ago, when their mother had been so upset about Margo taking off for New Jersey—and not just New Jersey, but a job that took her to all sorts of far-flung places where she was out of touch for months at a time. She'd argued that they all needed to get away from home, except for Caroline for some unfathomable reason, that Margo's desire to travel the world and capture it in photographs wasn't any different from her desire to throw beautiful parties for people in a beautiful, big, bustling city.

But now, when she thought of her own daughter wanting to do something like that—

It choked her up, imagining that one day her own daughter might want to go travel to dangerous places like that to follow her dreams.

What am I supposed to do? She wondered wildly, stirring the stew a little too hard. *Tell her that she can't?*

She could feel tears welling up by the time Aiden walked in, hanging off the edge of her lashes. She bit her lip, not wanting him to see how upset she was, but she could tell that he picked up on it as soon as he walked in.

"Hey there," he said softly, going to wrap an arm

around her waist and press a kiss to the top of her head. "What's going on?"

Nora set the spoon down in the cradle on the stove, turning to press her face into her husband's shoulder. "I'm happy to be having a baby, I really am," she sniffled. "But I can't help worrying. There are so many things that could go wrong. So many things we could do wrong. We can't protect her from everything. And we can't stop her from going out and wanting to be her own person, even if that means having a dangerous job like Margo. You know she's going to want to leave when she grows up, even if it's just for a while. That's normal, to want to leave home, but—"

She could feel herself breaking out into full-on tears, and Aiden squeezed her gently, rubbing her shoulders as he rested his chin on top of her head.

"You're worrying about things eighteen years from now," he said gently. "There's always the chance that she won't want to take off. Caroline didn't. I didn't. And if she does, we'll be understanding about it enough that eventually she'll come right back. If she doesn't, we'll make sure we're all on good enough terms that we stay in touch. We can't decide what kind of person this little girl is going to grow up to want to be, we just have to do our best to get her there in the right way. That's all we can do. The rest is up to her."

He turned his head a little so that he could see Nora's face as he added, "We need to enjoy each little bit as it happens. This part, right here, is what's happening right now. So we focus on that, and not what's going to happen when she's all grown up."

He reached down, tilting her chin up slightly so that he could give her a gentle, sweet kiss.

"I know you worry a lot, Nora. But it's all going to be all right. We've got your family, and each other, and pretty soon we're going to have the most perfect daughter anyone ever had."

Nora let out a sigh, sinking into his chest. "You're right," she said softly. "I'm sorry."

"There's nothing to be sorry about," Aiden said gently. "I'm just reminding you that we'll miss out on life if we spend all our time worrying, because sometimes you need the reminder. We all do. You should be enjoying this time with your sisters while they're all here."

He took a small step back, placing a broad hand on Nora's belly. "This baby is going to be loved by everyone and well-looked after. We've got that village you always hear about, for sure. You're not doing this alone in the slightest."

Nora gave him a small smile, her worries fleeing as she felt overwhelmed with gratitude. She'd picked the right man, for sure. And she felt so much happier now, surrounded by so much love.

He was right, she decided, turning back to the stove as Aiden went to start slicing up the bread to go with the stew. There was no point in spending all of her time worrying.

Everything was going to be all right.

CHAPTER SIXTEEN

Margo ran down her list as she set her supplies down on the counter at the general store, trying to make sure that she hadn't missed anything they needed for the fundraiser. Leon was ringing things up just as Bethany came out from the back room, holding the cutest Pomeranian that Margo had ever seen. It was fluffy and golden, with a puffy tail and tiny ears, and it immediately yipped at Margo the moment it set eyes on her.

"Hey there," Margo crooned at the dog, as Bethany approached. She'd always loved the idea of having a dog, but that was impossible when she traveled as much as she had for work. She'd made do by occasionally volunteering at the animal shelter to walk dogs when she was home, but those days were few and far between. "Is he yours?" she asked Bethany, and Bethany laughed, shaking her head.

"No, his owner is just late picking him up from his grooming appointment, so I get to snuggle him a little longer. Don't I?" she cooed, cuddling the dog to her chest. "Did Leon tell you that we're entering our tree in the decorating contest?" she added, glancing back up at Margo.

"No, he didn't." Margo grabbed a sleeve of maple candies and added it to the pile of supplies. Not strictly on the list, but after a morning of shopping, she wanted a treat. Also, she was getting thoroughly sick of being stuck on crutches, and that only added to her desire to get something to treat herself. "What's the theme? Or do you have any plan for it?"

Bethany grinned. "I'm not telling," she said, a glimmer of mischief in her eyes, and Margo shook her head.

"Not even a hint?"

"Not even a hint," Bethany said. "But it's going to be fantastic, I can promise you that."

"Everyone has been so excited about it," Margo said, as Leon started to bag up the supplies and she reached in her pocket for the inn's credit card. "I'm so glad to see that everyone has really wanted to help. I didn't expect that the idea would work, at first."

"Of course it worked!" Bethany exclaimed. "Everyone loves the inn, and they love your parents. We're all a family, a community. We wouldn't miss the chance to help, and this is a fun way of doing just that. What you and your sisters came up with is brilliant!"

The bell over the door chimed, just then, interrupting them, and Margo twisted around to see Rhett walking in.

"Hey there, Leon," he called out. "You got that case of Gatorade I ordered?"

"Sure thing. You mind coming around and grabbing it? It's a little heavy."

"A case of Gatorade?" Margo laughed, looking at her brother-in-law. "Did Caroline ask you to get that for the tree-decorating contest?"

Rhett chuckled. "No, it's for the firefighters. The annual holiday fireworks show is tonight."

"Oh," Margo said softly. "No one mentioned that. Where is it? That sounds like fun." It was a relatively clear day so far, and as long as it stayed that way over the evening she could picture it being beautiful. All those explosions of color this far out from the city, against the dark sky and over the snow. She'd never seen fireworks in a snowy place before, and she was suddenly very eager to experience it.

"It's up the hill just past the ski slopes." Rhett glanced at her crutches and winced. "Sorry."

"No, it's fine. I'm not traumatized just by the mention of the word 'ski'," Margo said with a laugh. "That's a bit of a hike for some fireworks."

"Well, it's a part of the tradition, or so I was told the first year I was here. The hike in the snow is all a part of the fun. Everyone brings hot cocoa thermoses and hikes up there together. It's a whole thing."

"That sounds really fun, actually. I assume Caroline is going. I should ask Mom if she's up for it. I really want to go."

Bethany hesitated, wrinkling her nose a bit. "Not to burst your bubble, but you're on crutches, honey. I go to that fireworks show every year, and it's definitely not something you can manage. Those crutches won't make it in the snow."

"There's got to be a way. I *really* want to go." Margo bit her lip, stubbornly trying to think of some way around her current situation.

This fireworks show was the first thing that had really caught her interest since she'd been home, and she didn't want to miss out on it. It seemed like an adventure, hiking up the snowy hills at night to see the fireworks, and more than anything, she disliked feeling like she was being held back when there was an adventure to be had.

"I'm sure I can figure something out," she insisted firmly.

"You don't want to get hurt again. Doctor Thorpe would say—" Bethany started, just as the bell over the door chimed again.

"What would I say?" Spencer asked as he walked in, and Margo spoke without thinking, so frustrated about the situation that she couldn't think it through.

"Spencer could take me!" she exclaimed, and there was a sudden, bemused expression on Bethany's face.

"Where am I taking you?" Spencer laughed, glancing over at Bethany. "There's a whole conversation I've missed out on, apparently."

"Margo found out about the firefighters' fireworks event," Bethany explained. "She really wants to go, but it's just not conducive to being on crutches. She's as stubborn as her sisters though," she added fondly, completely ignoring the frown on Margo's face at being talked over like she wasn't there.

Margo half expected Spencer to be annoyed that she'd volunteered him to help her get to the fireworks show without even asking. But instead, he just chuckled, glancing over at her.

"Of course I'll take you," he said easily. "What kind of doctor would I be if I let you go hobbling up the slopes *again* without supervision?" He grinned, then snagged the bag that Leon had just finished packing the supplies into. "Here. I'll take this out to the car for you."

Margo sighed as she followed him out, feeling guilty.

"I'm sorry," she said, as soon as they were out of the store and at the car. "I shouldn't have said that, and just assumed you'd take me. You probably have something else going on, or other plans, or work. I mean, I don't even know if you have someone else you want to go with. After all, I made it very clear that I wasn't staying here all that long, and—"

She stopped talking abruptly, realizing that her nervousness had made her start babbling. Spencer reached up, gently touching the tip of his index finger to her lips, a smile still on his face.

"I'm more than happy to take you," he said sincerely. "But we'll have to figure out some way to manage that. Bethany's right, that hike won't be easy with a broken leg. We'll have to be creative. But," he added as her face started to fall, "don't you worry. We'll find a way."

His smile spread, and Margo felt butterflies start to take off in her stomach.

CHAPTER SEVENTEEN

Friday evening, Spencer got into his car and headed out to a small ranch at the edge of Evergreen Hollow, where Jim, an elderly patient of his, lived. He knew Jim had a handful of horses on the ranch still, that he stubbornly kept taking care of despite the fact that he was starting to get to the point where it wasn't entirely feasible, and he'd had the beginnings of an idea, after leaving Margo at the general store when he'd found out how badly she wanted to go to the fireworks show.

He'd found out, in the past year, that Jim played Santa for the town every Christmas. He owned a sleigh that two of his horses were trained to pull, an honest-to-goodness wooden sleigh that the town decorated with ornaments and garlands every year. And he'd given Jim a call earlier that week, asking him if he might be able to borrow the sleigh and horses for something very important. After divulging a few details, Jim had been happy to oblige, all in the name of young love at Christmastime.

Spencer hadn't had the heart to tell him that it wasn't really *love*. Margo had made it very clear that she was leaving as soon as her leg was healed, and he had no plans to stand in the way of that. He wouldn't. She deserved to live her life however she wanted to live it, and it wasn't his place to tell her one way or another what that was. He knew her mother and sisters were privately hoping that his connection with her would keep her in Evergreen Hollow, but if he was being honest—

If she *were* to stay, and he truly didn't think she would, he would want her to stay because she thought it was the best thing for her. Because it was what she wanted for her life, not just for him. In his experience, that wasn't something that would work out well, in the end. And he'd rather she leave happy than stay and eventually be miserable because she'd felt boxed into it.

But for now, none of that mattered. He was good

at living in the moment and enjoying the good things while he had them. He'd learned that early on in medical school when his free time was limited, and the moments he got to himself were few and far between. He'd learned to really cherish those late night drinks with friends, the brief glimpses of life outside of books and exams. And that had only been underlined later on when he'd become a doctor, and he'd seen how many people lost their lives early to illness, accidents or other causes. He'd become all the more certain that life was to be enjoyed in the moments that made him happy, as they were happening, and that worrying about a future that wasn't certain would only mean missing out on all the good things happening right then.

So he truly wasn't worried about when Margo might or might not leave. All he cared about was getting to spend time with her now, while she was in Evergreen Hollow.

And he was absolutely insistent that he was going to pull this night off for her, this thing that she'd actually said she really wanted.

Jim was waiting outside on the porch for him when he got out of the car, waving cheerfully. "The sleigh is all ready for you," he said, pushing himself to his feet and ambling toward Spencer carefully.

"Horses are ready to go. Got a bit of pep in their step from the cold weather."

Spencer couldn't help but wince a little at that. "I'm a little nervous," he admitted. "I've never even ridden a horse before, much less driven a sleigh. Any tips?"

Jim waved a hand, chuckling. "Ah, you'll be fine. You can trust the horses, they know what to do. They're old hands at this."

Spencer laughed a little uncertainly. "I certainly hope that's true."

"'Round back." Jim gestured. "I can show you if you'd like."

"That's all right," Spencer said quickly, a little concerned about the idea of Jim out walking around in the snow. He was sure the older man did plenty of things around the ranch that he as a doctor wouldn't have advised, but he didn't see any reason to add to those things himself.

The horses and sleigh were waiting where Jim had said they would be, hitched to the sleigh just outside the barn and tied up to a post waiting for Spencer, a pretty black horse with a white blaze down its face and four white socks, and a slightly shorter bay with a deep black mane and tail, and a thin black stripe down its face. They tossed their heads and nickered as Spencer walked up, and he patted the bay's neck a little uneasily, hoping that he wasn't going to regret this decision.

It wouldn't help anyone if *he* joined Margo in having a broken limb.

But Jim was right. The horses knew what they were doing all on their own, without Spencer really needing to have a whole lot of input. They pranced merrily through the snow on the path that wound through the woods and along the roadway leading to The Mistletoe Inn, the small bells on the leather harness jingling. It lifted Spencer's spirits, and made him feel truly merry in every sense of the word. He felt sure that Margo would love the surprise.

He couldn't wait to see her face when she saw it.

* * *

Margo was upstairs in her bedroom with Nora, looking nervously at the clock as she hobbled around in an effort to get ready. She was already frustrated, because it took twice as long to do anything with her injury, and anxious about the night with Spencer on top of it. He'd reassured her that she hadn't overstepped, but she also hadn't been able to stop overthinking it, and she was beginning to be more and more certain that he'd just been saying that to be nice. That she actually *had* overstepped, and screwed everything up in the process.

"Here." Nora dug a dark green cashmere sweater out of Margo's drawer. "This looks great on you. And I can help you with your hair. I know you always like to do fun things with it. It's going to be cold, so make sure you wear a heavy coat."

"Maybe this was a bad idea," Margo interrupted, chewing on her lower lip as she leaned against the bed, hopping awkwardly into a pair of fleece-lined leggings.

With the cast, jeans were impossible, so she was relegated to leggings and sweaters or hoodies. Not her ideal outfit for a date, but she didn't have much choice. And Spencer *had* seen her at her absolute worst, a mess with a freshly broken leg, so maybe this was a step up, after all.

"He's probably annoyed that he has to figure out how to help a girl with a broken leg get up a stupid hill to watch *fireworks*, of all things," she said with a sigh. "He probably just felt guilty saying no, especially after he was the one who pursued me. But he's probably regretting that now."

There was a smirk on Nora's face, and Margo paused, narrowing her eyes at her sister.

"What?" she asked, and Nora chuckled.

"I was just thinking, the fact that you're so nervous shows that you're developing feelings for him. You wouldn't be so jittery if you weren't."

Margo pursed her lips, but she couldn't deny it. She *was* developing feelings for Spencer. He'd been kind and attentive, and if he wasn't thoroughly aggravated that she'd volunteered him for the fireworks show tonight and basically backed him into a corner about saying yes, he was an incredibly sweet guy for helping her do this.

On paper, he was a lot of things she'd always wanted: handsome, smart, successful, ambitious in his own right. But his ambition stopped at being a small-town doctor, and that was where the problem lay. Because for anything to happen between them, Margo would have to stay in Evergreen Hollow.

And she just couldn't see that being her plan for her future.

"You're going to have fun tonight," Nora said confidently, and as Margo pulled on the sweater and slipped a pair of small gold hoops into her ears, she sat down behind her on the bed to start braiding her sister's hair. "Spencer wouldn't have agreed if he wasn't excited about this too. I feel sure about that."

"I hope so," Margo said quietly, the slight tremor

in her voice betraying her nerves. Nora finished braiding her hair, looping it around behind her ears and securing it with pins, and just as she slid the last bobby pin into Margo's hair, the inn's doorbell rang.

"I bet that's Spencer," Nora whispered conspiratorially with a grin and slid off the bed. Margo followed, right behind Nora as they walked to the door, and she let out a small gasp as Nora opened it and she saw what lay just beyond.

Spencer was standing next to a sleigh. A real, honest-to-goodness sleigh, with horses and everything. She vaguely remembered old Jim having a sleigh and horses, using them for his Santa performance when she and her sisters were children, but she'd never imagined that *this* was how Spencer would pull off his promise. And he didn't look annoyed at all. In fact, he was beaming, clearly proud of his solution.

If anyone would have asked her before she returned home, back in her old office in New Jersey maybe, how she would have felt about a situation like this—she would have probably called it cheesy. Silly. Even if, deep down, she might have thought it was cute, she would never have admitted it.

But there was no part of her, in this moment, that thought that what she was looking at was anything other than the most romantic thing anyone had ever done for her.

Spencer walked up the stairs carefully, holding his arm out for Margo so that she could hobble down the few steps to where the sleigh was waiting. She leaned into him, and he gave her his full support, giving her the chance to feel just how strong he really was. He didn't have the build of the kind of man who spent endless hours in the gym, but something more functional, something she thought she liked much better. It made her want to lean into his chest and feel those strong arms around her, and she smiled at the thought of doing just that in a little while, watching the fireworks.

Nora was definitely right. She was absolutely developing feelings for Spencer Thorpe.

Spencer helped her into the sleigh, and she saw that there was a large, thick, soft, knitted blanket folded on the seat, big enough for two people to snuggle under it. He unfolded it, tucking it over her legs, and gave her hand warmers for her to tuck into her mittens.

"What do you think?" he asked, turning to her as he climbed into the sleigh and slipped under the blanket as well, tucking it around his legs so that none of the frigid air could seep in.

Margo smiled at him, her heart fluttering as she took it all in. "I had no idea you knew how to drive a sleigh," she teased, and Spencer chuckled.

"I don't," he admitted. "Jim told me the sleigh pretty much drove itself, and he was right. These horses know exactly what to do if I just sort of point them in the right direction. I'd be in trouble otherwise." He grinned at her. "But don't worry. We're safe in their hands. Hooves?"

"Definitely hooves." Margo snuggled a little closer to him, taking in his thick fisherman's knit sweater and jeans, just the edge of his sandy blond hair visible beneath the dark blue knit beanie he wore. There was a little stubble on his chin, a five o'clock shadow that he probably hadn't had time to shave before collecting the sleigh, and she liked it. It was more rugged than what she was used to, and she found it more attractive than she would have thought.

"This is all very romantic." Margo leaned into him, letting herself enjoy the moment as the sleigh slid gracefully through the snow, the bells jingling and the clop of the horses' hooves the only thing disturbing the quiet night air. "You really pulled out all of the stops."

"It was the best way that I could think of to get a

girl with a broken leg halfway up a mountain," Spencer teased, glancing over at her as he wrapped the reins around his fingers.

"And I definitely don't mind," he added quickly as if he could hear the echo of her worries from earlier. "I like problem-solving, you know. It's probably part of why I became a doctor. There's something really satisfying about someone coming in with an issue, and piecing together what's wrong and how to fix it. This was an easy problem to solve. And much happier than a lot of the ones I deal with." He smiled. "I've been looking forward to this all day."

"Me too." Margo let out a breath, watching it crystallize in the air in front of her. "I think I know that feeling. It's like getting the perfect shot—the one I see in my mind when I see something I want to photograph. All these places I've gone, I have to bring them home in a way that lets the people who read my articles feel attached. A way that makes them care, that transports them. And that feeling when it all lines up just right and I get the shot I want?" She smiled, feeling nostalgia for the last trip she'd been on. "It's such a good feeling."

"We both seem to have found our calling in life," Spencer mused. "It's lucky. Not a lot of people find that."

Normally, Margo thought, that was exactly the kind of thing that would have sent her on a spiral, wondering if she'd found and lost her calling, if she'd never get to experience that feeling again. If all her chances had run out with the loss of her job. But for the first time since Richard had given her the bad news, she just couldn't dwell on it. Everything around her was too beautiful, and the night was too perfect.

It was like something from a postcard. The kind of thing she would have taken a picture of if she had her camera, but she was glad she didn't, because she didn't want to miss a single second of any of it, even to snap a photo.

The dark silhouette of the maples against the starry, clear night sky was stunning. The snow was crisp, and the flutter of it in the air as the sleigh glided through it was a pleasant background noise as the horses' breath puffed in the air and the bells kept time with their strides. She put her hand on Spencer's knee over the blanket, and she saw him smile out of the corner of her eye.

She could hear voices as they got closer, and her excitement ramped up. She leaned forward, peering out into the darkness as Spencer guided the horses along the trail, carefully finding a spot among the other places where people had carved out spaces for chairs and blankets in the snow at the top of the hill. Margo saw Bethany and someone else she didn't know circulating with hot cocoa and apple cider, and Spencer glanced over at her.

"Want something?" he asked, and she nodded.

"A hot cocoa sounds wonderful."

He bought a hot cocoa for her, and a hot spiced apple cider for himself, thanking Bethany as she handed over the cups. Margo snuggled down under the blanket, wondering if she'd ever had a date as perfect as this before. If she had, she couldn't remember it. She couldn't think of anything she would have rather done.

She gasped as the fireworks began, bursting out over the dark, wintry night sky. They were all Christmas colors—red, green, yellow, white and blue —and she smiled as some of them exploded in the shapes of trees and stars, and finally, a sleigh.

"Just like ours," Spencer said with a smile, and Margo laughed, nodding as she leaned into him.

"Did Rhett tell you about that one ahead of time?" she teased, and Spencer shook his head.

"Honestly, I think I've only met him once or twice. He's the most responsible of the firefighters over at the station. Hardly ever has any injuries.

Actually, I think I've only ever seen him for checkups for his son."

"Caroline will be so happy to know that you described her husband as *responsible*," Margo laughed, taking another sip of her hot cocoa as more red and green fireworks exploded over the sky.

"I've been all over the world," she murmured, as they fizzled out, a cascade of blue and white following, illuminating the snow. "I've traveled to so many different places. And I don't think anything I've seen has made me feel quite like this before."

Spencer turned slightly to look at her, and she saw him raise a careful brow, his voice measured. "Could the company possibly have anything to do with it?" His hand slid over hers, his leather glove pressed to her soft knit mitten. "Because I know that for me, being here with you is making tonight even more magical."

Margo bit her lip, turning toward him to meet his eyes. Her heart sped up in her chest, and she knew this was a leap. A leap that could possibly end in a fall. But she'd been taking those all her life. Nothing, in this moment, felt more *her* than taking a chance— whether or not it ended in happily ever after.

"The company definitely has something to do with it," she whispered.

Spencer's hand tightened over hers, and he leaned in. A burst of red and green illuminated them both, as his mouth brushed over hers.

He kissed her, for the first time, as they both saw fireworks.

CHAPTER EIGHTEEN

Margo felt as if she were floating on a cloud as she walked into The Mellow Mug the next morning. She had planned to sit down with a cup of coffee and continue going over the details for the fundraiser, but she already knew that she was going to find it hard to concentrate. Her thoughts were full of Spencer and their date last night, along with that perfect, magical kiss; it was all she could think about.

She knew Melanie could see it on her face as soon as she walked up to place her coffee order. "All right, spill all the details," Melanie said, her voice teasingly demanding as she propped her elbows on the pastry case, clearly not intending to take any coffee orders until Margo complied. "I saw you riding in on that sleigh last night. I'm going to need to hear *everything*. That's the most romantic thing any man has ever done. That's movie-level romance, Margo. *Book*-level romance. So spill."

"It's nothing crazy," Margo tried to protest, but the look on Melanie's face told her plainly that Melanie wasn't buying it. "Okay, fine. Rhett came into Sugar Maple while I was getting supplies, and I found out about the fireworks show. I really, really wanted to go, but everyone kept telling me it was impossible with my bum leg." She gestured frustratedly toward the cast. "This thing is *really* getting on my nerves."

"Okay, but how does Spencer factor into this?" Melanie interrupted, and Margo laughed.

"I'm getting there. He walked into Sugar Maple just as I was saying that I *had* to figure out a way to go, and when I saw him, I just blurted out that he could help me figure out a way without really thinking about it. I was thinking he's a doctor, right? He'll have some solution."

"So you just *volunteered* him?" Melanie burst out into laughter, and Margo narrowed her eyes at her friend.

"Yes," she admitted, drawing the word out reluctantly. "I did. But he was such a good sport about it. I wondered if he'd regret it, or if he was secretly a little resentful about having to escort me around."

"Obviously not, because he got you a *sleigh*," Melanie pointed out. "So you're saying he thought of that all on his own?"

"He did," Margo said. "That was all his idea. I didn't even know Jim was still kicking, let alone that he still had the sleigh and horses. Spencer arranged the whole thing and surprised me. We rode up to the show, and snuggled under the blanket, and... he kissed me."

She felt her face flush a little, her heart racing all over again at the memory.

"We're definitely seeing each other now," she added. "I don't know for how long, with me needing to leave for work and all, but it's a thing. We're going to grab dinner soon."

"It all sounds perfect," Melanie breathed, ringing in Margo's usual latte order. "That's the most romantic thing I've ever heard, honestly."

"He is pretty perfect," Margo agreed. "But like I said—"

"Never say never," Melanie chided, slipping out a maple cinnamon roll and putting it on a plate. "You could always stick around, you know. Be the handsome town doctor's wife." She winked at Margo, who rolled her eyes.

"We just kissed for the first time *last night*. A little early for that, don't you think?"

Melanie just shrugged, with a mischievous smile, and went to make Margo's latte.

She'd blown off that suggestion quickly enough, but Margo had to admit that since last night, she had toyed with the idea of staying longer. Maybe not *forever*, but long enough to find out if this was really something between her and Spencer.

She didn't want to look back and wonder, or regret leaving so soon because she hadn't given it time to find out whether this was something that she really wanted. She wasn't getting engaged tomorrow, or anything—she'd thought about officially extending her vacation through the new year, and seeing how things went.

In the meantime, she could find some freelance work to pad her rapidly dwindling bank account. She had options, and it wasn't as if anyone was banging down her door with a job offer anyway. She could make the most of it, and see how things with Spencer went.

She felt a flicker of excitement at the idea, the first she'd had in a long time when the idea of being in Evergreen Hollow came to mind. But as soon as she settled in at a table with her cinnamon roll and latte, the door to The Mellow Mug opened, and her stomach dropped to her feet as she saw Chris Long walk in.

He looked exactly as she remembered, just older, the same as he had when she'd seen—and run from—him at the general store. Jet black hair, those dark brown eyes, tall with a woodsman's build and a full beard to complete the look. He'd really leaned into the rugged Vermonter aesthetic, and he looked like he was doing just fine. Thriving, even.

Her throat closed up as she watched him walk up to the register to order, Melanie's face carefully blank—ostensibly so that she didn't give away the fact that Margo was sitting across the cafe.

Margo thought it was probably too much to hope that he would get his coffee and leave without noticing her, and unfortunately, she was right. Chris turned as he waited for Melanie to make his coffee, his eyes casually sweeping over the cafe, and she saw the moment that he froze as he saw her sitting there.

His expression cleared instantly, back to that casual aloofness that made her feel so much worse as he collected his coffee, striding toward her. He looked like he was barely interested in the fact that she was there, and meanwhile, her heart felt like it was going to climb out of her throat. He was going to come *talk* to her, and she had no idea what on earth she was supposed to say. It had been a long time, and clearly he was over it. She should be too, but she just didn't think a hurt like that was so easily gotten over.

Chris flashed her a smile, the to-go cup of coffee in one broad hand. "Back in town, Margo? I thought I heard something about the third Stoker sister being back for the holidays."

"Just back for a few days," she clarified. "Or at least, that was the plan. I might stay longer. I haven't decided yet."

"Didn't your sister get married? That firefighter with a kid? You two should bring him by the farm sometime. We could catch up a little more, like old times. If you do end up sticking around a little longer, which seems pretty likely, considering..." He gestured at her leg. "Accident here?"

"The ski slopes," Margo muttered, her neck heating. She felt irritable all over, like her skin was crawling at his nearness, his familiarity. She was thoroughly disgusted by the idea that he seemed to think they could be friends, just because time had passed.

Not enough time had passed for her to forgive

him for what he'd done, and she didn't think it ever would. She gritted her teeth, hoping he wouldn't ask too many more questions. If he asked what she did for a living, she was going to lose it—she couldn't possibly admit that she'd come home because she'd lost her job.

"Just seeing family?" Chris asked, and she nodded quickly, hoping he'd accept that at face value. "That's nice. Holidays at home always are.'"

What else have you ever done for the holidays? She wanted to snipe. *Have you ever been in Alaska under the northern lights, or on a beach in Spain for Christmas? No? Didn't think so.*

But she couldn't, because then he would ask her about her job, and she would either have to lie or admit that she'd been laid off, which would undermine her point.

He hadn't said anything outright to make her feel any certain way, just been overly friendly and familiar, considering how they'd parted. But having him there, talking to her, all casual and confident, just made everything that was wrong come flooding back, dispelling her lighter-than-air mood.

It reminded her all over again that despite one perfect night, her life was actually falling apart. She was living in a room at her parents' inn, she was unemployed, and she was sitting in a small-town coffee shop with a broken leg. None of this was what she'd seen for herself a month ago. Two weeks ago, even.

"The farm is going great," Chris added, as if she'd asked. "It's hard to keep a farm profitable these days, but it's doing better than it did when I took over, actually. And I'm thinking I might propose to Kathryn over the holidays. A Christmas proposal is always a hit, I'm told."

He grinned at her, tipping his coffee cup toward her, as if there was anything cheery about the conversation. "Anyway, you look busy," he added, nodding at her notebook, and she couldn't tell if it was sarcasm or not. "I'll let you get back to it."

Margo felt sick to her stomach, as he started to walk away. All her thoughts of staying through the holidays, of seeing where things went with Spencer, of being open to new possibilities the way Caroline had suggested—all of it deflated instantly, like a popped balloon.

There was no way, she thought, that she could stay in a town where she would regularly run into him. And she *would*, because it was Evergreen Hollow, and even if Chris lived on the outskirts at his farm, everyone ran into each other all the time. It was impossible not to.

Furthermore, the last thing she wanted for her life was to have to actively avoid someone forever, which she would, because no one *ever* seemed to leave this place.

She'd been successful, before this. *She'd* left, and she'd done exactly what she'd wanted to do. This was a hiccup, but she needed to prove to herself that was all it was. Putting off really hunting for a new job, doing freelance work, all of that was just a way of putting off what was the most important thing, and always had been.

Spencer or no, broken leg or no, she needed to get back to traveling as soon as possible.

CHAPTER NINETEEN

Spencer checked his watch as he handed a prescription to his last patient of the day, seeing that it was five p.m. exactly. The clinic was about to close for walk-ins, and he didn't have any more scheduled patients. Short of an emergency, which happened occasionally—but not nearly as often as it had in San Francisco—he had the rest of the evening free.

He didn't want to seem too eager. But he hadn't been able to get Margo off his mind all day. Their date last night, for all his worries, had been perfect. The sleigh ride back and forth had gone off without a hitch, no pun intended, and it had all been so magical that he found it hard to believe he'd come up with it. It was something about Margo, he thought. He'd always been thoughtful, on the occasions he'd had time to date in the past, but there was something about her that made him want to go the extra mile. To be that truly romantic kind of man that he always heard that women swooned over. He wanted to wow her, to treat her the way she truly deserved, and make her feel as if she were the only woman in the world to him.

Truly, there wasn't any other woman who had ever made him feel the way she did. He had to remind himself that she wasn't sticking around, that anything they had together was temporary, and should just be enjoyed for what it was. But that was hard to keep in mind when he remembered kissing her in a horse-drawn sleigh under a spray of fireworks the night before.

Just text her, he told himself as the patient left, and he was alone in the exam room once again. He straightened up, heading to his office as he heard the receptionist leaving, and pulled out his phone

SPENCER: Hey there. How would you feel about dinner tonight? Rockridge Grill? I heard they have a duck leg special tonight that's to die for. Johnathon told me about it personally.

He paused for a moment, wondering if she'd get a joke over text, and decided to go for it anyway.

SPENCER: Maybe I could even text ahead and ask if he has any candles in the back. The nice ones.

A few minutes went by, and he felt a twist of anxiety. Maybe it was too soon. There were supposedly rules about this sort of thing, but he'd never paid attention to them, mostly because he'd never had the kind of schedule that allowed for it. But maybe Margo wanted to be given space. Maybe she wanted room to think things through before they went out again. Maybe all those rules mattered to her.

His phone chimed, and he grabbed it.

MARGO: Hey. Sorry, but I spent all day going over numbers and spreadsheets for the decorating contest and the roof at the inn, and helping Caroline with that since I can sit and do it, and she needs to be on her feet for other stuff. I'm really exhausted. Can we have a raincheck?

His heart plummeted. On the surface, everything about her text made sense, but he couldn't help feeling disappointed. He'd hoped that she would be riding the same high he was, that she would have been just as eager to see him after such a perfect night, but clearly, that wasn't the case.

She'd warned him that it was going to be casual, but last night had seemed anything other than casual. And he couldn't help wondering what had gone wrong.

It had all been so perfect. He didn't know what the problem was.

Which made it impossible to solve.

That evening, Nora climbed up into the attic of The Mistletoe Inn, looking for some boxes of Christmas decorations that her mother had remembered. She knew if Caroline was there, she'd have chided Nora for going up to the attic in her 'condition,' but Rhonda couldn't be climbing ladders after her hip replacement, and Donovan was out at his weekly pub meeting with his fishing buddies. It could have waited until the morning, of course, but Rhonda had been so excited, and honestly, Nora had been curious to see what she would unearth.

She couldn't find the boxes anywhere though. She had a feeling Caroline had probably done a purge at some point, and the old decorations— probably ones that didn't have a lot of sentimental value—had been a casualty. She did, however, find a photo album under the stacks of books and tangles of old Christmas lights.

Nostalgia tugged at her, and she slipped the book under her arm, heading back down the ladder and into the living room where Margo was sitting by the fire with a cup of peppermint hot cocoa, Rhonda's homemade marshmallows floating on top. "Mom brought in a cup for you too," Margo called out as she twisted around, seeing Nora walk into the room. "She said you should be down from the attic soon. Did you find the decorations?"

"No," Nora admitted. "I think Caroline probably got rid of them. But I did find this." She produced the photo album, sitting down next to Margo as she opened it. She wondered if Margo would resist the trip down memory lane, but instead, Margo picked up her mug of hot cocoa and scooted closer on the couch, readjusting so she would be comfortable with her leg stretched out on the ottoman.

"Oh look, there's Aiden," Margo said, as Nora flipped it open to a series of photos. "I still can't believe the two of you ended up together. I remember you saying he was cute back then, but you thought he didn't like you."

"I still thought that when I came back," Nora laughed. "But it all worked out in the end. I'm glad it happened now, and not back then. It was all the right timing."

She flipped through some of the pages, smiling as she landed on a spread of a "career day" event that the school had held. "Look at that," Nora said, pointing to where the three of them were standing. "Caroline didn't dress up at all, just wore her jeans and a flannel, so she got that right. And I wore a pencil skirt and one of mom's button-downs and a blazer, and you talked Dad into letting you bring his camera." Her finger rested on the photo, and she smiled at Margo. "Businesswoman and photographer. We really both did what we wanted to do, didn't we?"

She laughed as she said it, but she saw the lopsided smile that crossed Margo's face. "What is it?" Nora pressed, and Margo let out a sigh.

"This is nice," she admitted. "Going down memory lane with you, being back here in this cozy little town, feeling safe and surrounded by family. It feels different than it did back then, you know?"

"I do." Nora nodded. "I felt the same way when I came back. It wasn't so—suffocating, anymore."

"Except it still is, sometimes. Sometimes there are moments like sitting here with you with old pictures and hot cocoa or being up on a hilltop in a sleigh with Spencer watching fireworks, and I feel like I could really be happy here. And then something happens like running into Chris in the coffee shop—"

"You ran into Chris?" Nora interrupted, and Margo nodded.

"Yeah. And he acted like we were just old pals now. Like it was all water under the bridge from here on out. He suggested that Caroline and I bring Jay by the farm and talked about how well it was doing, telling me all about his *girlfriend*. Said he was thinking about proposing to her over the holidays. As if I would want to hear any of that."

She grimaced. "And that just reminded me how small this town really is, and how I would always run into him, and it brought back all the reasons I left. All the reasons why I needed the world to be bigger than Evergreen Hollow, you know? So I don't know if..."

Margo trailed off, but Nora thought she understood, that she could hear the rest of what her sister was thinking, because she'd been there too.

"I left here feeling like I wanted to get away from it too," Nora said quietly. "You know that. I wanted to escape just as badly. And I did, just like you. But when I came back... I don't know, my perspective has changed since then. It's nice to be in a place where everyone cares so much. The older I get, the less I like being as alone as I was in Boston. You know, I had my friends and my work colleagues and all of that, but it was always an effort to get together. And a lot of the time, the effort felt one-sided. My apartment was gorgeous and perfect, but so is my house here, just in a different way."

Nora let out a breath before continuing, a soft smile pulling at her lips. "You know, I was always afraid of what I'd be missing out on if I stayed in Evergreen Hollow. But then I came back and realized I was missing out on a lot by being gone too. So I had to decide what was more important to have in my life, and by then, well—it was all of the things here."

There was a long pause before Nora spoke again, the crackling of the fire filling the quiet. "I'm sorry I was cold to you at first," Nora said, glancing over at Margo with the photo album balanced between their laps. "I was hard on you for being gone for so long, but that wasn't exactly fair. I didn't come home all that often after I left either."

"I wouldn't have, if I hadn't lost my job," Margo admitted. "And I am glad I came back. At least for a little while."

"This place has a lot to offer, if you let yourself look at it with different eyes," Nora said quietly. "Through how our lives are now, not how they used to be. You've gone to so many different places and done so many cool things. Maybe now is a time to try something quieter. Maybe even fall in love," she added pointedly, and Margo gave a small laugh.

"I appreciate it," she said after a moment, taking a sip of her cocoa. "But I don't know if my heart is ready for that. Look how long it's been since Chris, and it still hurts seeing him. If things don't work out with Spencer, I just don't know if I want to go through that again."

"You're older now," Nora pointed out. "It won't be the same. It's different, going through heartbreak when you're an adult, instead of freshly out of high school."

"It still hurts. And you had a handsome carpenter to distract you after your engagement fell apart," Margo added. "I have unemployment and a very drab apartment."

It was blunt, but Nora had to concede that she had a point. "Still," she said, "you can't avoid it forever, just because it might hurt."

"I can. It's just whether or not I want to." Margo flipped a page in the photo album pensively, sipping at her cocoa. "I really don't know what I want, right now."

Nora could remember how that felt. And she could sympathize, remembering how worried she had been about risking her heart with Aiden.

But she hoped her sister would take the chance.

CHAPTER TWENTY

Spencer hadn't heard from Margo since their romantic date at the fireworks show.

At least—he had thought it was romantic. He'd thought she had, as well. But now he was second-guessing himself. She'd seemed so enthused by all of it, so happy. The way she had kissed him back had felt genuine. All of her reactions had felt genuine. But if she really had felt that way, why hadn't she so much as texted him since then?

It was frustrating. He wasn't used to feeling this way, and he didn't know what to do about it. If she'd really wanted him to leave her alone, he would have —he wasn't going to pursue someone who truly wasn't interested. But instead, he was left wondering, and he preferred certainty to that, even if the answer wasn't the one he wanted.

He had needed to drop off the tents for the fundraiser, and he kept an eye out for Margo as he did, hoping that he would see her at the pavilion where they were setting up. He spotted her leaning on her crutches near a fire pit that Leon was assembling, looking utterly adorable in a thick black cable knit sweater, dark-wash jeans, and a beanie with a fuzzy pompom tugged down over her hair, which she'd left down and in thick waves.

It was clear, even from a distance, that she looked happy. She was talking animatedly to Leon, and he felt a pang in his chest, because she seemed happier and more relaxed than she had since he'd met her. It seemed like she was settling into being back home, maybe even enough to consider staying. But if she *was* happy, and not just preparing for her exit at the first opportunity, then why hadn't she texted him?

He walked toward where she was standing, hoping to at least get some clarity. She seemed like she was in a good mood, and not in too much of a hurry, so he hoped she wouldn't blow him off. The fact that he had to wonder, after how good things had seemed, stung more than a little.

"Margo."

She jumped when he said her name, and he felt bad for not making his presence more obvious. He hadn't meant to startle her. She looked completely caught off-guard, and he cleared his throat, trying to seem more casual than he felt.

"What are you doing here?" she asked, and he frowned. He felt anything but casual, in this particular moment.

"The tents you asked me to source," he explained. "I was just dropping them off."

A moment of awkward silence hung between them, and he blurted out what was in his head before he had a chance to fully think it through.

"Why are you avoiding me, Margo?"

Out of the corner of his eye, he noticed Leon start to sidle away, giving them space.

Her eyes widened, and he thought he saw a faint, embarrassed blush bloom on her cheekbones.

"I'm not," she said, a little defensively. "I've just been busy. All this fundraiser stuff takes up a lot of time, and I've taken a lot of it on. Nora has so much going on with her work and getting ready for the baby, and Caroline practically runs the inn these days, and it's so busy this time of year. Meanwhile, I'm just... here. So I've been taking a lot of it on."

Spencer shook his head. "Margo, we're both

adults. Being busy doesn't mean you can't send a text message once in a while. You could have told me you wanted to see me but just couldn't get free. The fact that you didn't contact me is a message in and of itself."

Margo bit her lip, and he felt his heart sink a little.

"Look," he continued. "I get it. We said from the beginning that we weren't making any promises, and that this probably wouldn't be anything more than casually getting to know each other. You weren't planning on sticking around. But there was something between us, or at least, I thought there was. If you're finished with this, I at least deserve to hear it outright, instead of you just ghosting me."

He tried to keep his voice even as he spoke, and he held her gaze, trying to read her emotions in her expression. No one had ever drawn him in as thoroughly as Margo Stoker had, and before he let his heart get any more involved, he needed to know where they stood. He couldn't sit around and wonder what he meant to her. He'd rather know, one way or another, even if the answer disappointed him.

Margo's expression softened, her eyes shining.

"I wasn't finished with it," she admitted in a low voice. "After our date, I couldn't stop thinking about you. I was thinking about where this thing between us could go, honestly. I was hopeful. I thought maybe —" She broke off, chewing on her lower lip. "But it doesn't matter now."

Spencer frowned. "Why not?"

"I ran into Chris," she admitted. "Not even 'ran into,' that's not really the right word. I was just at The Mellow Mug trying to get some work done, and he walked in. He decided to talk to me and fill me in on everything he had going on, whether I wanted to hear it or not. And I realized that if I stayed here, that would be my life. Having to see Chris, that constant reminder of being hurt, and never being able to get away from any of it. It reminded me of why I left in the first place. And I just..." She sighed. "This town is way too small and full of too many bad memories for me, Spencer. And I didn't see any point in continuing to explore something with you when I'm going to leave."

"You could have at least told me that." He ducked his head to catch her eyes, that pang stinging in his chest again. "I was sitting around thinking I'd done something wrong."

"You didn't. I was just reminded of how much it hurt, the last time I let myself get really involved with someone here. It still hurts, if I'm being honest.

And I don't think I want to risk going through that again. But it's hard, because I really do..." Margo hesitated. "That night we had was wonderful. Maybe the best night of my life. But I don't see how we could have a future together if you're here in Evergreen Hollow and I'm not."

The hurt wormed deeper, the pang in his chest spreading.

"There was a spark there when we first met," he said quietly. "I know we both felt it. And we're always happy when we're together. We have fun. I would have hoped the possibility of what that could turn into could have overshadowed the past. Especially a past that's so long ago."

"It's not just that," Margo said, and the defensiveness was back in her voice. "I need my career too. I can't just *stay* here. What would I do? It's the antithesis of what I do for a living. And I need my work more than anything."

Whatever he'd been expecting her to say, it wasn't that. He felt like he'd been struck, and he reeled, staring at her as she propped herself up on her crutches.

"I'm sorry, Spencer," she said quietly, and he thought he saw genuine regret in her eyes. But that didn't change the fact that something he'd been so hopeful for was ending, just like that. Before they'd even really had a chance to make something of it, or even try.

He couldn't say anything. He couldn't think of what he would *want* to say. So he just watched as she hobbled after Leon on her crutches, suddenly numb to everything around him, including the cold.

He wasn't sure what he had thought would happen when he'd come to talk to her.

But he hadn't thought it would end like that.

CHAPTER TWENTY-ONE

The night that the Stoker family picked to decorate their tree for the fundraiser was Christmas-card perfect. The whole family was there: Rhonda and Donovan, Nora and Aiden, Caroline and Rhett and Jay, and Margo. They had decided to theme the tree around holiday baked goods, since Rhonda loved to bake so much, and she had made snacks for everyone that reflected it.

Donovan had built a fire, and there was mulled wine, apple cider, and hot cocoa with those amazing homemade marshmallows. Rhonda had brought two trays out, one with local charcuterie and crackers, local jams and honey and a small dish of pickles, and another tray of sweets—brownies, decorated sugar cookies, maple candy and peppermint bark. They had all found ornaments to fit the theme, along with what Rhonda already had, and everyone was excited to see what the others had picked out.

It was the perfect family holiday evening, and Margo was happy that she was there for it, but she couldn't entirely relax and enjoy herself, because she couldn't stop thinking about what she'd said to Spencer earlier.

The worst part of it was that he'd been right. She had been avoiding him, and for the worst reasons, because she hadn't wanted to come right out and say that she wanted to call things off. She hadn't been sure that she did. He was perfect in so many ways. He was handsome, and successful, and smart, funny and kind and romantic, everything she would have said she wanted out of a partner, if she was really looking for one. And right up until she'd run into Chris, she'd been giving serious thought to at least giving it a small chance.

He was right too, that what they had together should be more important than a heartbreak from so long ago. But it still felt so fresh, and she couldn't help but blame this place, Evergreen Hollow, that never changed and made everything that happened here feel like it never faded or went away either. All the bad was frozen in time along with the good, and she didn't know how to shake that feeling.

But if that was really how she felt, that she couldn't stay and that she didn't want to keep pursuing anything in the meantime, Spencer was right that he deserved to know that. She should have felt relieved that it was all said and done, that she could enjoy what little remained of her holidays with her family and then move on, back to the life that she was meant to be living.

She couldn't stop seeing the expression on his face when she'd said that she needed her career most of all though. He'd looked so hurt. He'd looked hurt throughout all of it, as if he didn't even recognize her. She felt like she'd disappointed him, and in a way, she felt like she'd disappointed herself too, for letting everything get to her so strongly that it upended the happiness she *had* found while she was home.

All of that, swirling around in her thoughts, made it hard to focus on the festivities.

"Look what I found!" Nora came downstairs, lugging another box, and Aiden quickly crossed the room to take it from her. "It's all those ornaments you sent us over the years, Margo, from all those different countries. There are almost certainly some things in here that fit the theme. Like this one!" She dangled a small ceramic strudel ornament from one finger, on a piece of red silk ribbon.

"Ooh, I want to see!" Jay exclaimed, making a beeline for the box. "These are all from other countries, Aunt Margo? That you went to *yourself*? That's so exciting!"

Margo laughed as he plopped down next to the box, walking over to sort through them along with the rest of the family that was gathering around. She'd forgotten a lot of what she'd sent over the years, so she was curious to see too.

"They are," she answered Jay, dropping down to the floor next to him. "I picked them all out myself. But I've been to so many different places, I need a refresher on what's in here too."

"Have you ever seen any places with fossils?" Jay asked, and Margo heard Caroline laugh as Rhett let out a groan. Jay's dinosaur and fossil obsession wasn't showing any signs of letting up anytime soon.

"Well..." Margo let out a slow breath. "One of the places I was possibly going to go before I came here was somewhere where a *lot* of fossils have been found. I was going to go explore it, and take a lot of pictures so that other people could see it too, and write an article so that they could read about it."

Jay frowned. "Why didn't you go? That sounds really cool."

"It would have been," Margo agreed. "But my job couldn't keep me, so I didn't get to go."

"That's a bummer," Jay said, picking up a small nutcracker out of the box. "But if you'd gone there, Aunt Margo, we wouldn't have gotten to see you for Christmas." His eyes widened, as if he were realizing something in that moment. "I might not have gotten to meet you at *all*. Caroline said you hadn't been back home in *years*."

She felt her heart twist at that. "You're right," she said quietly. "I hadn't been back in a very long time. So it's probably good that I was able to come back when I did."

"What's this one?" Jay pulled out a blown glass orange.

"That one is from Spain. It was handmade by an artisan who spent years learning how to blow glass. It's very fragile." She took it gently from him, handing it to Rhonda. "And this one..." Margo pulled out a knitted sheep. "This one is from when I was in the Alps."

"It's soft!" Jay squeezed it, before Caroline laughingly plucked it out of his hand. "And this?" He picked up a miniature beer stein.

"That's another one from Germany. I've been there a couple of times. And this one is from Japan." Margo plucked out a ceramic origami crane.

"Ooh, look at this one!" Jay took out a delicately crafted, old-fashioned replica of a tiny Mini Cooper. "This is so cool!"

"I got that in Italy. It was actually really funny, because I'd almost gotten into a wreck with one right before I went into that shop. It was like something out of a movie. My taxi was in traffic, and we started pulling forward, and he had to dodge this guy on a Vespa. And then this blue Mini Cooper came careening around the corner." Margo dodged to one side, knocking her shoulder into Jay's as he gasped and laughed. "It was going *so* fast. Just driving crazy. The taxi driver managed to swerve, and it went around us, like it was chasing the Vespa. I still have no idea what was going on with that—"

She broke off as she saw Nora suddenly drop the ornament she was holding back into the box, turning sharply on her heel and walking quickly toward the kitchen.

"Keep going through these, okay?" Margo said to Jay, pushing herself up off the floor and following Nora. She heard the sound of sniffling as soon as she got near the kitchen, and she walked in to see Nora wiping a sleeve over her eyes as she half-heartedly plated more cookies.

"Hey. What's going on?" Margo asked gently, walking up next to her sister. "I know I've been gone a long time, but—"

"It's not that." Nora gave her a watery smile, wiping a sleeve over her eyes again. "It's just... hearing those stories scares me, you know? Aiden told me I shouldn't worry so much about the future, but it's so hard."

"What scares you?" Margo turned, leaning back against the counter as she looked at Nora.

"Just that once my baby is born, I won't be able to protect her from the world." Nora sniffed again, picking at one of the cookies, crumbling it onto a napkin as she spoke as if she needed something to do with her hands. "I can't help thinking that she's going to grow up and want to leave like we did, and go out into the world. And what if she wants to go to places like all of these crazy cities you've been to? It's wonderful and exciting, I know, but it's also so dangerous!"

She broke off, her eyes welling up again, and Margo gave her a reassuring smile.

"It's just a sign that you're going to be a good mother, that you're worrying about it," she said gently. "But you'll protect her the best that you can, and you'll raise her to be smart and careful, and you'll be the best mother. But one day you'll have to let her spread her wings, just like we did, and she'll have to make some mistakes. And I'm sure that's really hard to watch. It was probably hard for our mom, and it'll be hard for Caroline when Jay gets older, and it'll be hard for you too. But she'll get really good, valuable life experience out of it."

"Is that how you feel?" Nora asked curiously. "Has all of that made a difference for you?"

"I mean, you moved to Boston. I'm sure you know how it feels too." Margo gave her a lopsided smile. "But I made mistakes along the way. I grew a lot as a person from traveling so much, I think. I definitely don't regret any of it. I learned so much about myself, and others. But—"

Margo hesitated for a moment, drumming her fingers against the edge of the counter before she continued.

"Staying so distant from everyone because of my hurt over Chris was a mistake. I regret that now. I could have been in contact more, come home more." She let out a long breath. "And how things ended with Spencer was another mistake, I think."

"Ended?" Nora stared at her. "What do you mean?"

"I told you about running into Chris." Margo tapped her fingers against the edge of the counter again. "Spencer was texting me, trying to set up another date, and I made excuses not to go. And then I just ignored him. I didn't want to break it off, because I like him, but I was scared. He saw me today at the site for the fundraiser, and he came over to talk to me. He was pretty upset, which was understandable."

"And you didn't patch things up?" Nora's eyes were round.

"No." Margo bit her lip. "I told him about seeing Chris. That this town felt too small and constricting after that. And that I needed my career. I basically said all of that was more important and that I would be leaving as soon as I could, without coming right out and saying exactly that." She winced. "He was upset, I could tell. I walked away, and he hasn't texted since. Which I don't blame him for, since I basically told him it was over and that I was leaving."

"Do you *want* it to be over?" Nora questioned, her worry about her daughter's future career choices clearly evaporating in the face of Margo's much more immediate difficulties with her love life. "Did you mean any of that?"

Margo shook her head. "I mean, small-town life *did* feel suffocating sometimes when I was younger. And seeing Chris really hurt. I don't know what I'm going to do if I'm not a photojournalist anymore. But I really, really wish I'd said it in a different way, and that we were still talking or trying to see where things between us might go. I wish I'd done it all differently, to be honest."

"Go talk to him," Nora urged.

Margo's eyes widened. "What, right now?"

"Yes, right now. Go over to his house and talk to him."

"Just show up?" Margo shook her head. "I can't do that."

Nora put her hands on her hips. "He got a sleigh and horses to take you to a fireworks show. You can show up at his house. Just *go*, before it's too late and you've let him get away. You don't want that, do you?"

Margo shook her head. "I don't. But we're decorating the tree, and—"

"They'll understand. Mom will *definitely* understand. Just go find him, sis."

Margo knew her sister was right, and she

couldn't argue. The longer she waited, the more settled it would be, making it harder for her to fix things. She needed to talk it out with Spencer, if only so that it wouldn't end like that. He deserved better, that was for sure. They both did.

"Aiden or Rhett can drive you—" Nora started to say, but with the decision made, Margo suddenly felt that she couldn't get there fast enough.

She couldn't wait for someone else to bundle up and pull a truck around and all of the explanations that would follow that.

She needed to talk to Spencer as soon as possible.

"No, that's okay," she said quickly. "I'll get there on my own."

Without wasting another second, she grabbed her crutches and headed for the back door.

CHAPTER TWENTY-TWO

For his contribution to the tree-decorating contest, Spencer had decided to do a *Gray's Anatomy* theme. It was a little on the nose, maybe, but he had a feeling a lot of the entries would be. He'd even gotten a 007 ornament off of Etsy, which no one would get if they hadn't watched the show. But even if no one understood it, it would be his own private little joke.

He hadn't really put a lot of effort into decorating a tree in years, but he'd gotten a local Christmas ale from the general store and takeout from Rockridge Grill, put his favorite Christmas jazz on, and he was having a good night. It was almost enough to soothe the hurt of his last conversation with Margo.

Almost.

It was hard not to think about her when he was decorating a tree for her family's fundraiser. But he was trying to put her out of his head as best as he could.

He would have thought he would have gotten better at that, after years of romantic disappointments caused by his job and the punishing schedule he'd had in San Francisco, but it felt worse now. Maybe because here, he felt that he finally had a chance at real love, and it still wasn't working out.

He reached for a small microscope ornament, and nearly dropped it when a knock at the door almost made him jump out of his skin.

"Just a minute!" he called out, setting down both his beer and the ornament and heading for the door.

He wasn't sure who he'd expected to see on the other side, but he was utterly shocked to see Margo there, red-cheeked and windswept, her hair tumbling out of her beanie around her face and balancing on her crutches on the snowy doorstep.

"Hey," she said uncertainly, and he just stared at her for a moment.

"Margo?" He wasn't quite sure that he wasn't imagining things.

"That's me." She bit her lip, shivering a little and he craned his neck to look around her, looking for some sign of a car. But there was nothing—just Margo Stoker, on crutches on his doorstep.

"How on earth did you trek through the snow?" He was still stunned, at a loss for words, latching on to the most immediate question. The idea of her making her way to his house on foot was utterly ridiculous, and extremely ill-advised on her part— and yet, unless he really was imagining things, there she was.

She lifted one shoulder in a lopsided shrug, her smile equally lopsided. "I just did. I—I have something important to tell you."

It jarred him enough for him to realize that she was still standing on his doorstep in the snow, probably freezing, and he winced, embarrassed that it had taken him this long to invite her in. "Come inside," he said quickly, stepping back and holding the door wide so that she could walk in, as a bit of the snow blew in over the entryway. "You're going to freeze."

Margo hesitated for a moment, then hobbled into the foyer, waiting for him to close the door behind her.

"I've got a fire going in the living room," Spencer said, gesturing for her to follow him. "And some of that local brewery's ale in the fridge, if you want one. I was just working on..."

He trailed off when he saw her standing stock-still just inside the living room doorway, her mouth fallen slightly open as she looked at the tree he'd been decorating.

"Spencer—" She blinked as if it was her turn to be in shock. Her gaze roved over the tree, as if taking in the clear theme and the pile of similar ornaments on the coffee table waiting to be hung. "Do you just like themed Christmas trees, or is that for the fundraiser?"

He laughed a little at that, although it was slightly hollow. "It's my tree for the fundraiser."

"But..." She touched one mittened hand to her mouth, her gaze flicking between him and the tree. "We argued. You're still participating in the fundraiser even after everything I said to you?"

He could hear how touched she was, just from the sound of her voice, and he nodded.

"You've worked really hard to make it a success, Margo. I want to be a part of that, to support it."

"I—" She blinked, biting her lip, and he could see the mingled confusion and emotion in her expression.

He stepped a little closer, turning to face her, his chest tight.

"How we left things was confusing," he admitted quietly. "And I won't lie and say that I wasn't hurt. But it doesn't change how I feel about you."

The misty look in her eyes instantly welled into tears, and she let out a small, hiccupping sob as she started to cry.

"I'm so sorry," she managed. "That's what I came here to talk to you about. I shouldn't have said that about my career. I shouldn't have ignored you after our date at the fireworks show. I handled all of that wrong, and I'm so sorry."

She sniffled and took a second to gather herself, drawing in a shaky breath before she continued.

"I like you, Spencer." Her voice was soft as she looked up at him almost shyly. "A lot. I've liked you since that awkward night when we met at the clinic after my accident. I was just in such a bad headspace, and I know it doesn't excuse anything, but I—"

Another tear rolled down her cheek, and Spencer couldn't stop himself from stepping forward to brush it away.

"Sit down," he said gently, motioning to the couch. "I'll get you a drink, and we'll talk."

Margo nodded, tears still sliding down her

cheeks, and he handed her a tissue before he went to get her one of the ales, returning to sit down next to her on the couch.

"Now," he said, popping the cap off of the ale and handing it to her. "Tell me what you came here to say."'

Margo took another deep breath.

"My job has been my whole life since I left Evergreen Hollow right after high school," she said quietly. "I needed to prove to myself that I would be fine without everything that I left behind. And I was. I had a really great time. I was good at my job. So when I lost it, it felt like I'd also lost my whole identity. I was already so embarrassed about the circumstances that made me come back here. And honestly, meeting you—it helped."

She bit her lip. "I started seeing things differently. Thinking about them differently. But I didn't know how to reconcile that with how I've lived my whole life. And then I ran into Chris the day after our date, and I realized how much that still hurt, and it all came back."

She paused for a moment, taking a sip of the ale and wiping the back of her hand over her eyes.

"You told me a little about that." Spencer hesitated. "Do you want to explain more?"

Margo waited for a moment, but she nodded. "He—we—we were together in high school. We got engaged on graduation night. We were going to get married, stay in Evergreen Hollow, the whole thing. A part of me wanted to leave, to go off to college and pursue photography and a career, but I thought I loved him so much."

She took another slow breath, her voice gaining a bit more strength as she went on. "He went to go help on his grandparents' farm for the summer. I stayed here, with my family. And I ended up finding out, while he was gone, that he was seeing someone else. She didn't know about me at all, or that he was engaged, or anything like that. It wasn't her fault. But I was crushed. And all I wanted to do was get away from here."

Spencer's eyes widened, a flash of anger on her behalf rushing through him. "Oh my gosh, that's awful. I'm so sorry that happened to you."

Margo gave him a small smile, her lips quivering a little.

"Thanks. Seeing him again brought all of that back. How hurt I was, and how completely blindsided I was—just as blindsided as I was when I lost my job a couple of weeks ago. But I can get another job. And I guess it reinforced that feeling of needing to show that I'm fine on my own. I was afraid of being stuck someplace where I would have to deal with that feeling over and over, and that I might get hurt again."

She trailed off, and Spencer shook his head, his chest tight. His heart was breaking for her, hearing the whole story. It made it easier to understand how she had reacted the other day, why she'd avoided him instead of telling him the truth about how she felt.

"I wish you had talked to me from the start," he said gently. "But I can only imagine how hard and confusing that must have been, especially when everything is in so much upheaval for you right now. I honestly—" He shook his head, reaching out to take her hand in his, both of theirs resting on her knee. "I don't know how anyone could have done that to you. It's unfathomable to me. And maybe this doesn't matter now, but I want you to know I would never do that. Not to you, or to anyone."

"I believe that," Margo said softly. "You're a good guy, Spencer. I knew that as soon as I met you. It's not that I think you'd intentionally do anything to hurt me, but sometimes relationships just don't work out, you know? Not because either person is bad, but just because they don't, for way more innocuous reasons than what happened with Chris. And I haven't had a real relationship since then, so I guess I was scared of feeling that way again, for any reason. It felt safer to just focus on what I knew, getting another job and getting out of here, rather than something that would require a different kind of leap."

"Sometimes you have to take chances." Spencer nodded. "I took a big one, coming here from San Francisco. I might've hated it, being a small-town doctor, leaving all the rush and responsibility of a big hospital behind." He smiled. "And although sometimes I do miss it, there are a lot of advantages here that I didn't have before. Parts of life I was losing out on that I have now. I'm glad I made that choice. But I know what you mean about not having real relationships. That's one of those things I was hoping would change, coming here, eventually. Back then, there was no time for it."

Margo bit her lip, nodding thoughtfully. "I told myself that I didn't really date because it was too hard to hold anything down when I was always hopping from one country to the next. But coming back here made me face the fact that that was really just an excuse to cover up how afraid I was of getting hurt. And I wasn't ready to face it when I kind of got smacked in the face with it, running into Chris like that."

"I understand," Spencer said quietly. "I know it wasn't personal, not hearing from you. And I'm glad you came to talk to me about it now."

"That's what I really wanted to do," Margo said, wiping the last of the tears off of her cheeks. "I wanted to tell you that I realized, after the last time we talked— things with Chris really messed me up emotionally. I had to face just how much. But I don't want it to still affect me so badly. I don't want to let it keep controlling the choices I make. And the fact of the matter is, before I got blindsided by it all over again, after our date, I could imagine a life with you. Even here, in Evergreen Hollow. I... still can." She paused, giving him a small, tentative smile. "I can still imagine that."

It took him a moment to absorb what she was saying. It felt like an entire weight was being lifted off him, like everything had lit up at once, and he leaned in on impulse, his hand cupping her cheek as he pulled her in for a kiss.

She leaned into it immediately, her other hand wrapped around his, and he thought as she kissed him back that there couldn't have been a more perfect moment. It felt like the kiss in the sleigh all over again, except it was just the two of them this time, with the glow of the Christmas tree and the crackling of the fire as their backdrop.

"I'm so happy to hear that," he said softly, as Margo sat back. The tight feeling in his chest was gone, replaced by something lighter, happier, as if his heart was more full than it had been in a long time. "I feel like the luckiest man in the world right now."

He reached up, brushing a lingering tear away from her cheek with his thumb. "Do you want to help me finish the tree?"

Margo laughed, still a little shakily. "Is that cheating, since I'm running the fundraiser?"

"Not if we don't divert from my very carefully planned theme. I already know where every ornament goes. You just have to hang them exactly where I say."

"I'm terrible at following directions," Margo said, and Spencer chuckled.

"Well, we'll just have to practice. What do you say?"

"Honestly? That sounds amazing." She took his hand, letting him help her up so that she could perch on the edge of the couch, near enough to the tree to hang ornaments on one side of it. The Christmas jazz vinyl that Spencer had put on earlier had run out, and he got up to switch it, the music filling the room as he handed Margo the microscope ornament that he'd nearly dropped earlier.

"Right there," he said, gesturing to a branch in front of her, and she followed where he was pointing, perching it in the perfect spot. "Exactly! See, you're a natural."

"I haven't decorated a Christmas tree in a long time," she admitted, as he handed her a small, sparkly blue ball ornament. "Wasn't much point, when I wasn't really at home this time of year often."

"I haven't either. For similar reasons, except I was always at the hospital so much that I didn't have time to decorate, and it seemed like a bit of a waste. But now I have my own house, and plenty of time. So I plan on having a tree every year, from here on out. And," he added, turning toward Margo to give her another soft kiss, first on the mouth and then on the tip of her nose, "I would love for you to help me decorate it. You can even pick out the theme next year."

"I like chaotic trees," she admitted, sliding the ball onto the branch he pointed out. "The ones where you collect ornaments over time, and it becomes less and less cohesive every year."

"Is that chaos, or a collection of memories?"

"That's true," Margo said, taking another of the small glass ornaments from him. "I like that way of looking at it."

He looked at the tree, and he could imagine it next year, empty and waiting to be filled with the first of their memories. He could see Margo in this space, year after year, or maybe a slightly different one that they'd pick out on their own.

It was fast, he knew, perhaps too soon to be thinking those kinds of thoughts, but she'd said she could see a life with him too. And he knew how short life could be, just as easily as it could be full and long. He saw no reason to waste time playing games when he knew who he wanted.

Especially when it was clear now that she wanted him too.

CHAPTER TWENTY-THREE

A day and a half later, Spencer still felt as if he were floating on air.

He and Margo had gone out for dinner the next day, and he'd taken her to Marie's, wanting to treat her to something special. They'd enjoyed a romantic dinner and good wine, and had gotten to know each other a little better, avoiding topics of exes or what Margo would do if she did plan on staying. They would have to talk about all of those things eventually, but right now, he wanted to enjoy the moment, and he knew that she did too. He wanted to enjoy the fact that things were good between them again, before they had to start working through the parts that would be harder.

And there was so much that was good. So much

to get to know. They'd talked about their lives, Margo's travels and Spencer's days as a doctor at a big hospital, trading exciting moments and misadventures and their favorite memories, until the server had come by to tell them that the restaurant would be closing soon. They'd gone to the only bar in town after that, a little pub attached to the brewery, and stayed until they'd closed too, before he'd finally given her a ride home.

He'd never met anyone before that he could talk to so easily, who was so full of life and stories, who was both interested in all he'd done and could hold his interest just as easily. The truth was that Margo wasn't like anyone he'd ever known before, and he was incredibly glad to have met her. He was even more glad to have had the chance to be more to her, and her to him. To have the chance at having a real relationship with her, that she was who he'd finally found, now that he could try to do exactly that.

He walked into Rockridge Grill to get lunch, still thinking about the night before. He didn't have much time—he'd called in an order instead of sitting down to eat, because he had an appointment immediately after his lunch break. But the to-go orders were backed up as well, and as he leaned against a booth to wait for his name to be called, he saw Chris Long sitting at a booth a few feet away, talking to another man that he vaguely recognized as being someone who worked at the feed shop in town. He didn't have livestock, but he thought he remembered the man coming in to get a thumb stitched after cutting his thumb opening feed sacks.

He'd known who Chris was as soon as Margo described him. The man had been in the clinic a handful of times over the past year, for various farming-related injuries. He had a pretty good recollection for names, something he'd picked up over his years as a doctor, and so he knew Chris by sight as soon as he saw him.

He also couldn't help overhearing their conversation. They weren't exactly being quiet about it, and the moment he heard Margo's name, he couldn't force himself not to listen.

"I can't believe she's back in town," the other man said. "It's been years. Out of the three of those Stoker girls, she's the one everyone really thought would never come back."

Chris snorted. "She wouldn't have, if she hadn't had to crawl back with her tail between her legs. But that's what she gets for running off and getting some ridiculous degree. Like taking pictures was ever going to be a sustainable job."

Spencer felt his shoulders tense, hearing that. Deep down, he knew he should stay out of it, that all of this was none of his business. But he was striding toward the booth before he could stop himself, his jaw clenched tight.

"Taking pictures kept her in a job and traveling all over the world for fifteen years," he said tightly, crossing his arms over his chest as he stared down at the two men. "You might think your job is more practical, but it didn't teach you not to treat women like trash, did it? At least Margo is a decent person. She's not the one who cheated on her fiancée and lied to the person she promised to spend the rest of her life with. And she's certainly not the one who is sitting here gossiping about his ex, minimizing all the hard work she did to get out in the world and make something of herself."

"Man, I don't know what you're talking about, but—"

Spencer kept talking, as if Chris hadn't tried to interrupt.

"Don't bother trying to deny it. She's told me what happened between the two of you. And honestly? It wouldn't matter if her career did crash and burn, even though it hasn't, because it's not that big of a deal for someone to have to switch jobs.

Doesn't mean their whole career was a waste. But as great as that career is, her value as a person isn't lessened if she's not doing it. It's not *her*. And clearly, you never saw her for the gem that she is, because you screwed that up royally from the very start."

He felt a little rush of satisfaction at the way Chris's mouth dropped partially open, his expression seemingly stunned by the intensity of Spencer's defense on Margo's behalf. Spencer could see the wheels turning in the other man's head as he tried to come up with a retort, but he shook his head, not giving Chris time to respond.

"Margo always deserved better than you," he said firmly. "Leave her alone from now on, do you hear me? She shouldn't have to deal with you badgering her on top of everything else, not when it's your fault she's not in your life any longer. That's your issue to deal with, so don't make it her problem. Understood?"

Spencer took a step back, glancing toward the counter as the woman there called his name, and he started in that direction, not bothering to give Chris another look. When he did glance back after grabbing the paper bag, he saw Chris throwing a couple of twenties onto the table and standing up, muttering something quietly to his friend as they headed for the door.

But that wasn't the only thing he noticed.

Caroline Stoker was sitting at a booth near the window with half a sandwich and a notebook in front of her, and she was looking right at Chris. Her gaze flicked to Spencer, and he tensed, realizing she'd seen the whole exchange.

He started to walk toward her, to talk to her about it before she could say anything to Margo. But before he could make it more than a couple of feet in her direction, she was already up and out of the door.

Margo had spent most of her afternoon at the fundraiser site, getting last-minute things ready before the big day. She was in the middle of directing a couple of the local guys in the process of setting up the tents when she saw Caroline headed her way. She waved a hand, starting to hobble toward Caroline, only to pause when she saw the look on Caroline's face.

"Did something happen?" she asked as her older sister caught up to her, frowning. "You look—

preoccupied, I guess. It's not something else at the inn, is it?"

Her stomach dropped a little at the possibility. She felt confident that the fundraiser was popular enough that they would be able to solve the issue of the roof, but they didn't need something else going wrong so quickly.

"No, not that," Caroline said quickly, waving a hand.

"What's going on, then?" Margo sank down on a nearby bench, and Caroline followed, her gloved hands tucked between her knees.

"I was just having a bite to eat at Rockridge Grill, and I saw Spencer."

Margo frowned. "And?"

That drop in her stomach sank a little lower. She trusted Spencer, but Caroline looked like she had something to say, and that small part of her that was afraid of getting hurt again twinged.

"Chris was there too, having lunch with a friend." Caroline hesitated. "I didn't hear their conversation, but I guess it must have had something to do with you, and Spencer must have overheard it. He went over there and told Chris off. Pretty emphatically."

"What?" Margo's eyes widened. "What did he say?"

A small smile quirked up the edges of Caroline's mouth. "A lot. He said that you'd worked hard at your career, and that it didn't matter that you'd lost your job, that it happens, and it didn't make you a failure. That you were still a good person, whereas Chris was trash for hurting you and lying to you, and that at least you didn't screw up the best thing to ever happen to you. He told Chris to leave you alone for good," she added, the smile spreading. "He was very insistent about that. That you shouldn't have to deal with him any longer."

Margo felt her eyes widen even further, a small shock running through her. She'd always thought of Spencer as very mild-mannered, and the fact that he'd defended her so forcefully was making her heart race. If he was there right then, she thought, she'd kiss him for standing up for her. A few weeks ago, she would have adamantly said that she didn't need or want anyone to defend her, that she could take care of herself. But she realized that she liked it. In this one instance, at least. She liked that he cared enough to do that. It meant more to her than she would have ever guessed that it would.

"Wow," Margo said softly. "I wouldn't have pictured that happening."

"It did," Caroline confirmed. She frowned a little, a small line appearing between her brows. "You don't seem upset by it. I thought you might be. You're always so independent. We all are, all three of us, in our different ways," she mused. "But I thought you might be upset that Spencer caused a scene with Chris."

"I would have thought so too, before this," Margo admitted. "But it makes me feel good, honestly. Like he really cares. He didn't have to get involved, but he did. He stood up for me. It's nice not to have to do it myself for a change. For someone to have my back. I guess..." She hesitated. "After getting tossed aside by Chris, it feels good to have a guy I care about be on my side."

Caroline's eyebrows shot up. "*Care about,* hmm? Do you want to elaborate?"

A dozen thoughts ran through Margo's head all at once, and she chewed on her lower lip.

"I like him a lot," she admitted, her heartbeat picking up its pace again.

"Nora said she thought you had some pretty strong feelings for him. But no one wanted to pressure you into feeling like you needed to stay. We all worried you might regret it if you left though. The two of you..."

Caroline trailed off, and Margo thought she could imagine what her sister might have been about to say.

Her heart raced faster and faster as she realized in a rush just how deeply her feelings really did go. How much she really did care about him, more than she'd wanted to admit at first. But after patching things up, and the date the night before, and now this—

Her feelings were so much deeper than she could ever have anticipated.

"I'm falling in love with him," she whispered, turning to look at Caroline. "I was so scared to say it out loud, or even think it, because it's so fast. But he's the best man I've ever met, and he brings out the best in me. He's perfect for me."

She expected Caroline, the most responsible and careful of all of them, to caution her. To tell her not to lose her head, or to not rush into anything, to be cautious and not fall head over heels into something that could hurt her.

But instead, her sister just smiled at her, the broadest smile Margo had seen from her in a long time. Maybe ever.

"You always make up your mind on things quickly," Caroline said. "And in a lot of people, that's a flaw. But with you, it's always served you well. It might have meant we all had to miss you for a long time, but you've always known your own mind. It's never steered you wrong. And I don't think this is any different."

"You don't?" Margo asked, surprised, and Caroline shook her head.

"I don't," she confirmed. "And I'm really, really happy for you."

Caroline leaned forward, pulling Margo into a hug, and Margo returned it after one brief, startled second. She knew, in that moment, that everything had gone exactly as it should.

It had been hard to lose her job, when it had been everything to her for so long. But she wouldn't have come back, otherwise. And she was so very, very glad that she had.

She had missed her family. She had been lonelier than she'd realized.

And now that she was home, she thought that there were a lot of very good reasons not to leave again.

CHAPTER TWENTY-FOUR

Spencer's stomach was so tied up in knots, he thought he might be sick. He knew in a town as small as Evergreen Hollow, there was no way that Margo wouldn't find out about what had happened at Rockridge Grill. It would get around, one way or another, and it would be so much worse if she found out from someone other than him.

It wasn't as bad as Chris cheating on her, not by a longshot, but he knew that wouldn't be the part that mattered if she found out from someone else. It would be that he'd tried to hide it from her, and he'd promised to be honest with her. Not to lie or omit things. He knew that honesty was what she needed out of a relationship, after what she'd had to deal with in the past. And he had to give that to her, no matter how difficult it would be.

He had to own up to what happened, and clear the air.

His appointments for the day couldn't be finished fast enough. It was hard to focus on his work, but he did his best to apply himself, knowing that mistakes as a doctor could have much worse consequences than just an administrative error. He put the altercation out of his head as best as could, but he knew he needed to go straight to see Margo, as soon as he was free.

The moment his last appointment for the day was over, he hung up his coat and hurried out to his car, before the receptionist and nurses had even left for the day. He was usually the last one out, but he couldn't wait any longer.

He headed straight for The Mistletoe Inn, hoping she would be there. He felt relieved when he saw her bundled up on the front porch, snuggled in a thick sweater under a knit blanket in one of the rocking chairs, with a steaming cup of something clutched in her hands. As he walked up the steps, he smelled chai tea.

As anxious as he was about her reaction, he was glad that he had at least found her. She didn't look angry, so he thought maybe he'd gotten to her first. He couldn't be sure, but he was hopeful that at the very least, even if she had already heard, the fact that he was coming to her and coming clean would matter.

He'd wanted to defend her, but the truth was, he'd acted on impulse. He hadn't really thought about the consequences, something that he never did. He thought it said something about how much he felt for her, but he also understood that she might not see it that way. And the last thing he wanted was for something to come between them again.

"Can we talk?" he said quietly, and Margo nodded.

It was hard to read her expression, and he felt that nervous twist in his stomach again. He sank into the chair next to her. It was frigid out, and she had the only blanket, but he didn't care. He just needed to talk to her.

"Did you hear about what happened?" he asked.

She nodded again. "I did." Her face was still impossible to read.

"I'm sorry. It just... it made me angry, to hear him talking about you like that. Like he deserved better than you, when the truth is that you've always deserved better than him. And the thought of him continuing to talk about you like that, while you're here, knowing that you said it made it harder for you to want to stay—"

He broke off, knowing that he was rambling, trying to defend what he'd done, and unsure if any of it would matter.

"I got carried away," he admitted. "I know that. I'm sorry if I crossed a line, and I would understand if you never wanted to speak to me again."

Margo's face had been perfectly calm and composed while he'd been speaking, giving nothing away, but as he finished, her eyes went wide.

He froze, shocked, as she set her cup down with a *thud* and threw the blanket back, pushing herself to her feet. He stood at the same time, uncertain, and was utterly startled when she threw her arms around his neck, pressing one hand to the back of his head as she kissed him deeply.

"I'm not angry," she said softly a moment later as she pulled back, breaking the kiss. "I'm really not. Hearing that you defended me like that? It meant the world to me."

"It did?"

He blinked at her, trying to process what she'd just said. That hadn't been what he'd expected at all.

Margo nodded. She was still standing very close

to him, her arms looped around his neck, and he was no longer cold, although the temperature hadn't changed at all.

"I care about you so much, Spencer, and knowing that you care about me enough to want to stand up for me like that? It means everything. I've never met anyone who's made me feel the way you do. I think... I think I'm falling for you," she whispered softly.

Her eyes met his as she finished speaking, the same nervousness that he'd felt earlier reflected in her face.

His pulse stuttered. He knew what it meant for her to admit something like that, to say it out loud. How far she had come since the day they'd first met, for her to let herself feel it. His heart swelled with the possibilities, with everything that unfurled in front of them with that knowledge that she was allowing herself to feel that way, despite all of her fears and reservations.

"What do you mean?" he asked softly, wanting to hear it again. Needing to hear her explain.

He had to make sure that he hadn't misheard, because this meant everything to him. The woman in front of him was everything he had ever wanted, and more.

Margo hesitated, and his heart skipped a beat again, for a different reason this time. He thought that maybe his fear had been right, that she hadn't meant it the way he'd heard it. But then she dropped her gaze, looking down at the small space of porch between their feet, and he realized she was nervous.

Her wide blue eyes came back up to meet his, and the look in them made warmth bloom in his chest.

"I'm not just falling for you," she said softly. "I've already fallen. I'm in love with you, Spencer."

There was no doubt or hesitation in her voice, and her words sent Spencer's heart soaring.

He picked her up without thinking, spinning her around in a circle, feeling as if he'd been given everything he'd ever wanted in one split second. He spun her again before setting her back down onto the porch, brushing her hair back with both hands as he looked down into her eyes.

"Say it again," he murmured.

"I love you," she repeated, never breaking his gaze even for a moment, and Spencer felt like his heart might burst.

"I love you too."

He brushed his thumbs over her cheekbones, not wanting to let her go. Not all that long ago, he thought he was going to have to do exactly that, and going to have to be okay with it in the end, because it was what she needed. And now she was standing here in front of him, telling him that none of that would be necessary. That she would be his.

"I'm the luckiest man in the world for having met you," he murmured, brushing his hands over her hair again, her arms still around his neck. "You're the most incredible woman I've ever met. Every single moment of my life has been better since I met you. Everything I hoped I'd find one day—someone who challenges me, who is smart and curious and fun and makes me laugh, someone beautiful and vivacious— that's all you, Margo. Every bit of it. I'm so lucky that you love me too."

"I feel lucky," she whispered, leaning against him. "I've never been with someone who makes me feel so loved and supported and accepted, just the way I am. You were willing to let me go, rather than change me. And weirdly enough—" She huffed a small laugh. "That made me want to stay. You want me for *me*, and that's all I've ever really wanted from someone else."

"I love you exactly as you are," Spencer affirmed. "I never want you to change a thing."

"I really am glad you stood up for me to Chris," she murmured. "I wasn't angry at all. I liked it."

He raised an eyebrow, a smile on his lips. "You'll always have a defender in me," he promised.

As he kissed her again, he knew he would do anything that he needed to in order to keep her right there in his arms.

CHAPTER TWENTY-FIVE

By the time the day of the fundraiser rolled around, the butterflies in Margo's stomach still hadn't stopped flapping around.

She felt giddy and light, floating on the happiness of having told Spencer that she loved him and hearing it in return, and it had infused everything she'd done. For the past few days, getting everything ready, she'd felt as if nothing could possibly go wrong, ever again.

It had been a long time since she'd felt that way.

The event center, where they'd set up for the fundraiser, was the most Christmas-y thing she'd ever done. But she had to admit, it was perfection. Nora had handled a lot of the decisions when it came to decorating, so of course, it was stunning, and

Caroline had handled the behind-the-scenes, paperwork stuff that Margo found horribly boring and impossible to concentrate on. She'd put it all into motion, arranged and delegated and pieced it all together, which was her strong suit—*doing* instead of planning, which had worked out perfectly in this instance.

In fact, if anyone had asked her a month ago if she and her sisters would have been able to work together almost effortlessly on a project, especially one this big, she would have laughed in their face. But it had brought them closer together, instead of pushing them apart, the way she previously would have thought.

The outside of the event center was set up with the booths she'd arranged, a pancake station and build-your-own hot cocoa and hot apple cider bars, surrounding a big fire pit with Adirondack chairs assembled around it. Twinkling garlands were hung around the outside of the building, with a holly arch in front of the door, leading into the interior, where it smelled thickly of pine and glittered everywhere with lights.

The rafters were strung with lights, the fireplace at the far end decorated, complete with stockings hung, and the Christmas trees that everyone had decorated and entered were lined up on one side of the building, each with a small tag with the names of the person or family who had entered it. On the other side, there was a buffet table filled with food, a few tables with handmade crafts, as well as pies, jerky and other food items for sale, the proceeds of which would all be donated to go toward fixing the roof of The Mistletoe Inn.

Margo pressed a hand to her chest as she took it all in, overwhelmed by what everyone had done for her family. She had always known that Evergreen Hollow residents supposedly took care of each other, but she hadn't really believed in it, hadn't fully understood what it meant until right then. That her parents would be taken care of, supported, just the way they'd done for the community their whole lives. She had no doubt that this would be a success, and that, by the end of the evening, the roof would no longer be a worry.

The event center was filling up, everyone milling around to look at the trees, clutching mugs of cocoa and cider. Margo could hear the sound of kids outside, laughing and playing in the snow, and she thought wistfully of Nora's baby, who would be there with the family the following Christmas. A

Christmas she would be in Evergreen Hollow to see, now that her plans had changed.

Spencer walked up behind her, wrapping his arms around her waist, and she jumped a little, then relaxed back against him.

"Everyone is so excited," she said, feeling a hum of satisfaction at how clearly happy everyone was with the event.

The residents of Evergreen Hollow were all talking excitedly about which tree they thought would win, commenting on the different ornaments, browsing the tables. She could feel the hushed anticipation in the air as they waited for the appointed judges, Sabrina Burns from the *Gazette* and her husband, to go around and survey the trees, and announce who had won first, second, and third place.

Sabrina, with her puffy red hair and cat's eye glasses, finally walked to stand in front of the fireplace, her husband standing next to her in his khakis and sweater vest. "Third place," she said, drawing it out as she surveyed the excited crowd, "goes to the Stoker family tree."

Margo gasped, thrilled, and she heard Nora let out a small squeak of excitement next to her. Even

Caroline had a broad smile on her face, and Jay was jumping up and down, clapping his hands.

"Second place," Sabrina continued, "goes to the fire department's tree."

Jay squealed again, clapping his hands. He had loved that tree in particular, Margo knew, even more than the Stoker tree. It had been spray-painted red, something he'd gotten to help with under Rhett's watchful eye and was fire-truck themed.

"Caroline *and* Dad won!" he enthused, and Margo laughed.

"Well, placed," Caroline said, but she was grinning, and so was Rhett.

"And first place..." Sabrina drew out the last word, adding extra emphasis, clearly thrilled to be the one presiding over the event. "Goes to the Kennedy's tree!"

Margo heard Bethany let out a squeak of glee, saw her kiss Leon enthusiastically before going up with Rhonda and the fire chief to collect their prizes. She'd seen Bethany's secret tree that morning when she'd brought it in, a ridiculously sparkly Grinch-themed tree, and she wasn't at all surprised that it had won. It had been a lot of fun, and absolutely over the top in the best way.

"I'm sorry your tree didn't place," she said,

turning to look at Spencer, and he shrugged, a smile on his lips nonetheless.

"It's more than all right," he said. "After all," he added, looping an arm around her waist and bringing her in for a kiss, "I got the girl. That's the best prize." He tapped her nose with the tip of one finger, giving her a quick kiss there as well. "And the best Christmas present ever."

Margo went up on her tiptoes, kissing him again, the scent of pine and homemade pies and the crackling fireplace filling her senses, making her feel warm and cozy all the way through. "Want to get some cider?" she asked, and Spencer nodded.

"Of course I do."

They walked outside into the frigid afternoon, Spencer sweetly tucking her scarf in a little more closely around the collar of her coat, and headed over to the apple cider station. Margo ladled some into a mug, adding cinnamon and whipped cream, and turned to see Sabrina standing just behind her, in her bright green peacoat.

"I heard you might be staying in town," Sabrina said as Margo took a sip of her cider, and she stifled a smile. If anyone would have heard that particular tidbit of gossip, it would be Sabrina. She was sure that Sabrina had heard the rest too, about Spencer chewing Chris out in the middle of Rockridge Grill, but Sabrina tactfully didn't mention it. Not that Margo would have cared if she had.

"Yes," Margo said, nodding. "I'm going to be sticking around for a while."

"Well, unless you've found any other employment opportunities, I have an offer to make you." Sabrina beamed. "Your mother told me all about your degree in journalism, and that you're adept at photography too. What would you think of coming to work at the Gazette?"

Margo stared at her for a brief second, before nodding enthusiastically. "Yes!" she said quickly. "Absolutely. I would love that—thank you!"

"You can start on Monday, if you like?" Sabrina smiled. "We can get you set up in an office and go over everything, give you a tour and let you get settled in. Not as exciting as I'm sure you're used to, but we stay steady."

"That sounds great," Margo assured her. "Monday is perfect. I'll be there."

Out of the corner of her eye, she saw Spencer beaming at her, a smile wreathing his face from ear to ear. He stepped up next to her, squeezing her mittened hand as Sabrina walked away, and she could feel his support, how happy he was for her, how perfectly all of the pieces had fallen into place.

She would never have believed this was possible. It hadn't been all that long ago that it had felt like everything was falling apart. But now she felt happy and content, down to her bones, as if her life were better than it had ever been before. She had a new job, an amazing boyfriend, and her family close by for the first time in a long time. And just in time for Christmas.

It was all perfect.

It was the start of her new life.

CHAPTER TWENTY-SIX

Four Months Later

Spencer sat in the cramped waiting area of the bustling Burlington hospital next to Margo, with Caroline, Rhonda, and Donovan sitting across from them. It felt a little strange, being in the waiting room of a busy hospital instead of in the middle of the action, but he wanted to be there to keep Margo calm.

They'd already been there for what felt like an eternity to him, even though he knew how these things went. He'd done a rotation through the maternity ward when he was in medical school, and he'd been reassuring Margo and Caroline, just as Rhonda had, that it was normal that it was taking a long time. After all, Nora had only been in labor for a few hours.

Everyone was on edge, anxious anticipation hanging in the air as they all awaited the arrival of the newest member of the family, and Margo squeezed his hand constantly. He knew how bad she was at sitting still. It had been hard enough to get her to follow her care instructions when she'd been in the cast, and the minute he'd gotten it off and her leg was healed, she'd been off like a rocket, never slowing down. He had worried, at first, that she'd realize that Evergreen Hollow was too small and confining for her after all, but that hadn't happened. Everything had continued to be perfect, just as it was now.

And Margo, even though she was clearly nervous, had a visible excitement about her. She'd integrated back into life in Evergreen Hollow without issue, finding happiness and passion in her job at *The Gazette*, even though it was so much slower-paced than what she used to do. He'd seen her find pleasure in the slower pace, just like he had, even though his job had once been much more thrilling than what a small-town clinic offered. She'd learned to enjoy the benefits of having a home, and regular hours, just as he had.

He watched her eyes dart nervously back and

forth between her family members, her excitement palpable, and he felt a warm satisfaction at the thought that Margo would be here for this new expansion of her family, that he would get to share in it with her, and that everything had come together better than he could have ever hoped. It made him happy in ways he'd never known were possible.

The fundraiser for The Mistletoe Inn's roof had been a smash success, and he had been thrilled to share in the joy of seeing the beloved town landmark repaired, celebrating along with Margo and the rest of the Stoker family. He knew it was a weight off her parents' minds to have the roof fixed.

After a little while longer, a nurse came out to meet them, clearing her throat. "You can come back and see Mrs. Masters and the baby now," she said, and they all shot up at once, ready to go back and see Nora and the new little one.

Aiden was in the room with Nora, standing next to the bed, the doctor saying something to them that Spencer couldn't quite hear. He was too focused on Margo, on her radiant expression as she saw her sister and the small bundle in her arms.

"We picked out a name," Nora said, leaning her head against her husband's arm tiredly.

"Madison Sophia."

She looked exhausted, but her eyes were shining with the look that Spencer had seen before, on other mothers in his rotation on maternity, completely drained from labor but still over the moon with happiness.

Margo's face lit up, and she walked to Nora's bedside, handing her the teddy bear that she'd been clutching since she left the house. It was soft-looking with brown fur, and the word *No matter where you roam* were written in a curling pink script in a heart on the belly.

Nora's eyes welled up as Margo tucked it in next to her. "Madison has such a courageous and adventurous aunt to look up to," she said softly. "And I couldn't be happier that she's going to get to grow up with you here."

Spencer saw Margo look over at him, meeting his gaze with hers in a meaningful glance, and his heart swelled.

Together, he and Margo had finally found a reason for her to put down roots. For her to slow down, as much as she ever could, and find happiness in one place. And while he had been happy in Evergreen Hollow before, nothing could match the joy that he'd found in sharing his life with her.

In that moment, he was overwhelmed with

happiness and contentment, everything as perfect as he could have imagined. And it would only get better, in time.

He couldn't wait to see what the next Christmas would bring.

The series continues in *Mistletoe and Memories*!

ALSO BY FIONA BAKER

The Marigold Island Series

The Beachside Inn

Beachside Beginnings

Beachside Promises

Beachside Secrets

Beachside Memories

Beachside Weddings

Beachside Holidays

Beachside Treasures

The Sea Breeze Cove Series

The House by the Shore

A Season of Second Chances

A Secret in the Tides

The Promise of Forever

A Haven in the Cove

The Blessing of Tomorrow

A Memory of Moonlight

The Saltwater Sunsets Series

Whale Harbor Dreams

Whale Harbor Sisters

Whale Harbor Reunions

Whale Harbor Horizons

Whale Harbor Vows

Whale Harbor Blooms

Whale Harbor Adventures

Whale Harbor Blessings

Evergreen Hollow Christmas

The Inn at Evergreen Hollow

Snowflakes and Surprises

A Christmas to Remember

Mistletoe and Memories

A Season of Magic

The Snowy Pine Ridge Series

The Christmas Lodge

Sweet Christmas Wish

Second Chance Christmas

Christmas at the Guest House

A Cozy Christmas Escape

The Christmas Reunion

For a full list of my books and series, visit my website at www.fionabakerauthor.com!

ABOUT THE AUTHOR

Fiona writes sweet, feel-good contemporary women's fiction and family sagas with a bit of romance.

She hopes her characters will start to feel like old friends as you follow them on their journeys of love, family, friendship, and new beginnings. Her heartwarming storylines and charming small-town beach settings are a particular favorite of readers.

When she's not writing, she loves eating good meals with friends, trying out new recipes, and finding the perfect glass of wine to pair them with. She lives on the East Coast with her husband and their two trouble-making dogs.

Follow her on her website, Facebook, or Bookbub.

Sign up to receive her newsletter, where you'll get free books, exclusive bonus content, and info on her new releases and sales!

Made in United States
Cleveland, OH
02 March 2025

14811966R00152